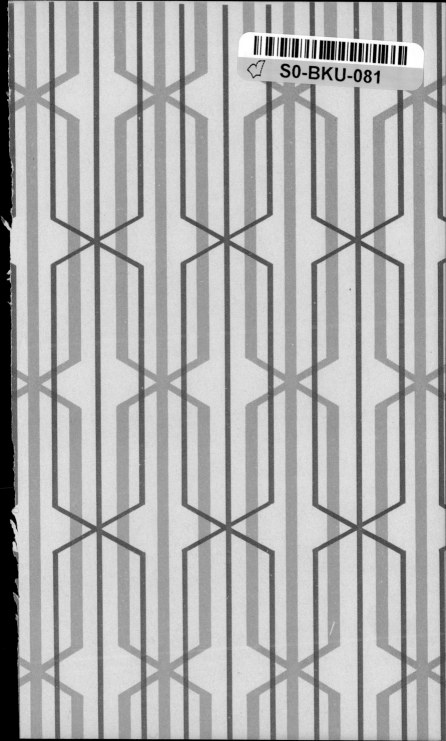

The Outcasts

And other Stories

THE OUTCASTS

And other Stories

BY MAXIM GORKY

Short Story Index Reprint Series

BOOKS FOR LIBRARIES PRESS
FREEPORT, NEW YORK

First Published 1905
Reprinted 1970

STANDARD BOOK NUMBER:
8369-3393-1

LIBRARY OF CONGRESS CATALOG CARD NUMBER:
75-113664

PRINTED IN THE UNITED STATES OF AMERICA

CONTENTS

THE OUTCASTS

THE OUTCASTS

I

THE High Street consists of two rows of one-storeyed hovels, squeezed close one against another; old hovels with leaning walls and crooked windows, with dilapidated roofs, disfigured by time, patched with shingles, and overgrown with moss; here and there above them rise tall poles surmounted with starling houses, whilst the roofs are shaded by the dusty green of pollard willows and elder bushes, the sole miserable vegetation of suburbs where dwell the poorest classes.

The windows of these hovels, their glass stained green with age, seem to watch each other with the shifty, cowardly glance of thieves. Up the middle of the street crawls a winding channel passing between deep holes, washed out by the heavy rain; here and there lie heaps of old, broken bricks and stones overgrown with weeds, the remains of the various attempts made from time to time by the inhabitants to build dwellings; but these attempts have been rendered useless by the torrents of storm-water sweeping down from the town above. On the hill nestle, amongst the luxuriant green of gardens, magnificent stone-built houses; the steeples of churches rise proudly towards the blue heavens, their golden crosses glittering in the sun.

In wet weather the town pours into this outlying suburb all its surface water, and in the dry weather all its dust, and this miserable row of hovels has the appearance of having been swept down at one of these moments by some powerful hand.

Crushed into the ground, these half-rotten human shelters seem to cover all the hill, whilst, stained by the sun, by the dust, and by the rains, they take on them the dirty nondescript colour of old decaying wood.

At the end of this miserable street stood an old, long, two-storeyed house, which seemed to have been cast out in this way from the town, and which had been bought by the merchant Petounnikoff. This was the last house in the row, standing just under the hill, and stretching beyond it were fields, ending at a distance of half a verst from the house in an abrupt fall towards the river. This large and very old house had a more sinister aspect than its neighbours; all its walls were crooked, and in its rows of windows there was not one that had pre-served its regular form; whilst the remnants of the window panes were of the dirty green colour of stagnant water.

The spaces between the windows were disfigured with discoloured patches of fallen plaster, as if time had written the history of the house in these hieroglyphics. Its roof, sagging forwards towards the street, increased its pathetic aspect; it seemed as if the house were bowing itself towards the ground, and were humbly waiting for the last stroke of fate to crumble it into dust, or into a deformed heap of half-rotten ruins.

The front gates were ajar. One side, torn from its hinges, lay on the ground, and from the cracks between the boards sprang grass, which also covered the great desolate yard. At the farther end of this yard stood a low, smoke-blackened shed with an iron roof. The house itself was uninhabited, but in this mean shed, which had been a forge, was installed a common lodging-house or doss-house, kept by a retired cavalry officer, Aristide Fomitch Kouvalda.

Inside, this doss-house appeared as a long, dark den, lighted by four square windows and a wide door. The brick unplastered walls were dark with smoke, which had also blackened the ceiling. In the middle stood a large stove, round which, and along the walls, were ranged wooden bunks containing bundles of rubbish which served the dossers for beds. The walls reeked with smoke, the earthen floor with damp, and the bunks with sweat and rotten rags.

The master's bunk was on the stove, and those in its immediate neighbourhood were looked upon as places of honour, and were granted to the inmates who rejoiced in his favour and friendship. The master spent the greater part of the day seated at the door of the shed in a sort of arm-chair, which he had himself constructed of bricks, or else in the beerhouse of Jegor Vaviloff, just across the way, where Aristide dined and drank vodka.

Before starting the lodging-house, Aristide Kouvalda used to keep a servants' registry office in the town; and glancing farther back into his life, we should find he had had a printing establishment; and before the printing business, according to his own account, he lived — and "lived, devil take it, well; lived as a connoisseur, I can assure you!"

He was a broad-shouldered man of about fifty, with a pock-marked face, bloated with drink, and a bushy, yellow beard. His eyes were grey, large, audaciously gay; he spoke with a bass voice, and almost always held between his teeth a German china pipe with a curved stem. When he was angry the nostrils of his red crooked nose would dilate wide, and his lips would quiver, showing two rows of large yellow teeth like those of a wolf. Long-handed and bow-legged, he dressed always in an old dirty military overcoat and a greasy cap with a red band, but without a peak; and in worn felt boots reaching to his knees. In the morning he was always in a state of drunken stupor, and in the evening he became lively. Drunk he never could be; for however much liquor he stowed away, he never lost his gay humour.

In the evening he might be seen seated in his brick arm-chair, his pipe between his teeth, receiving his lodgers.

"Who are you?" he would ask, on the approach of some ragged, depressed-looking individual, who had been turned out of the town for drunkenness or for some other reason.

The man would reply.

"Show me your papers, to prove that you are not lying!"

The papers were shown, if there were any forth-coming. The master would push them into his shirt, not caring to look at their contents.

"All right! For one night two kopecks; a week, ten kopecks; a month, twenty kopecks; go and take your place, but mind not to take anyone else's, or you will catch it. The people who live here are particular."

The new-comer would ask him, "Can one get tea, bread, and grub? Don't you sell them?"

"I sell only walls and roof, for which I pay the rogue Petounnikoff, the owner of this hole, five roubles a month," Kouvalda would explain in a business-like tone. "People who come to me are not used to luxury, and if you are in the habit of guzzling every day, there's a beershop just opposite. But you'd better get out of that bad habit as soon as possible, you skulker; you are not a gentleman born, then why do you want to eat? You had better eat your-self!"

For these and like speeches, uttered in a pre-tended severe voice, but always with a laugh in his eyes, and for his attention to his lodgers, Kouvalda was very popular among the outcasts of the town.

It sometimes happened that a former client would come into the doss-house, no longer ragged and down-trodden, but in more or less decent clothes, and with a cheerful face.

"Good-day, your honour; how are you?"

"All right; quite well; what do you want?"

"Don't you recognise me?"

"No, I don't."

"Don't you remember last winter I spent a month with you, when you had a police raid and three were taken up?"

"Oh, my good fellow, the police often come under my hospitable roof!"

"And, good Lord! don't you remember how you cheeked the police officer?"

"Well, that will do with recollections; just say simply what you want."

"Let me stand you something. When I lived with you, you were so"——

"Gratitude should be always encouraged, my friend, for we seldom meet with it. You must be a really good fellow, though I can't remember you; but I'll accompany you to the vodka shop with pleasure, and drink to your success in life."

"Ah! you're always the same—always joking."

"Well, what else can one do when one lives among a miserable set like you?"

Then they would go off, and often the former lodger would return staggering to the doss-house. Next day the entertainment would begin anew; and one fine morning the lodger would come to his senses, to find that he had drunk away all that he possessed.

"See, your honour! Once more I am one of your crew; what am I to do now?"

"Well, it's a position you can't boast about, but being in it, it's no use crying," argued the captain. "You must look at your position with equanimity, my friend, and not spoil life with philosophising and reasoning. Philosophy is always useless, and to philosophise before the drink is out of one is inexpressibly foolish. When you are getting over a bout of drinking you want vodka, and not remorse and grinding of teeth. You must take care of your teeth, otherwise there will be none to knock out. Here are twenty kopecks; go and bring some vodka and a piece of hot tripe or lights, a pound of bread, and two cucumbers. When we get over our drink then we'll think over the state of affairs."

The state of affairs would become clear in two or three days, when the master had nothing more left of the four or five roubles which had found their way into his pocket on the day of the return of the grateful lodger.

" Here we are, at the end of our tether!" the captain would say. " Now, you fool, that we have drunk all we had, let us try to walk in the paths of sobriety and of virtue. As it is, how true is the saying, 'If one hasn't sinned, one can't repent; and if one hasn't repented, one can't be saved!' The first commandment we have fulfilled; but repentance is of no use, so let's go straight for salvation. Be off to the river and start work. If you are not sure of yourself, tell the contractor to keep your money back, or else give it to me to keep When we've saved a good sum I'll buy you some breeches and what is necessary to make you look like a decent, tidy, working man persecuted by fate. In good breeches you will still stand a good chance. Now be off with you!"

The lodger went off to work on the towpath, down by the river, smiling to himself at the long, wise speeches of Kouvalda. The pith of the wisdom he did not understand, but watching the merry eyes, and feeling the influence of the cheerful spirit, he knew that in the discursive captain he had a friend who would always help him in case of need.

And, indeed, after a month or two of hard work, the lodger, thanks to the strict supervision of the captain, found himself in a pecuniary position which enabled him to rise a step above that condition into which he had fallen, thanks also to the kind assistance of the same captain.

" Well, my friend," Kouvalda would say, critically inspecting his renovated acquaintance, " here you are now with breeches and a coat. These matters are very important, believe me. As long as I had decent breeches I lived as a decent man in the town; but, damn it all! as soon as these fell to pieces, I fell also in the estimation of mankind, and I had to leave the town and come out here. People, you fool, judge by the outer appearance only; the inner meaning is inaccessible to them, because of their innate stupidity. Put that into your pipe and smoke it. Pay me half your debt if you like, and go in peace. Seek and you will find."

" How much, Aristide Fomitch, do I owe you ? " the lodger would ask confusedly.

" One rouble and seventy. You may give me the rouble or the seventy kopecks, whichever you like now ; and for the rest I'll wait for the time when you can steal or earn more than you have now."

"Many thanks for your kindness," replied the lodger, touched by such consideration. "You are— well, you are—such a good soul; it's a pity that life has been so hard on you. You must have been a proud sort of eagle when you were in your right place."

The captain could not get on without grandiloquent phrases. "What do you mean by being in my right place? Who knows what his right place should be? Everyone wants to put his neck into someone else's yoke. Judah Petounnikoff's place should be in penal servitude, but he walks freely about the town, and is even going to build a new factory. Our schoolmaster's place should be by the side of a nice, fat, quiet wife, with half a dozen children round him, instead of lying about drunk in Vaviloff's vodka shop. Then there's yourself, who are going to look for a place as a waiter or porter, whereas I know you ought to be a soldier. You can endure much, you are not stupid, and you understand discipline. See how the matter stands! Life shuffles us up like cards, and it's only now and then we fall into our right places; but when that does happen, it's not for long; we are soon shuffled out again."

Sometimes such farewell speeches would serve only as a preface to a renewed friendship, which would start with a fresh booze, and would end with the lodger being surprised to find that he had nothing left, when the captain would again treat him, till both were in the same state of destitution.

These backslidings never spoilt the good under-

standing on either side.   The aforementioned schoolmaster was amongst those friends who only got put
on his feet in order to be knocked over again.   He
was intellectually the most on a level with the
captain, and this was perhaps just the reason that,
once having fallen to the doss-house, he could never
rise again.

He was the only one with whom Aristide
Kouvalda could philosophise, and be sure that he
was understood.   He appreciated the schoolmaster
for this reason, and when his renovated friend was
about to leave the doss-house, having again earned
some money with the intention of taking a decent
room in town, Aristide Kouvalda would begin such
a string of melancholy tirades, that both would re-
commence drinking, and once more would lose all.
In all probability Kouvalda was conscious of what
he was doing, and the schoolmaster, much as he
desired it, could never get away from the doss-house.
Could Aristide Kouvalda, a gentleman by birth, and
having received an education, the remnants of which
still flashed through his conversation, along with a
love of argument acquired during the vicissitudes of
fortune—could he help desiring to keep by his side
a kindred spirit ?   It is always ourselves we pity
first.   This schoolmaster once upon a time used to
give lessons in a training school for teachers in a
town on the Volga, but as the result of some trouble
he was expelled ; after that he became a clerk at a
tanner's, and was forced, after a time, to leave that
place as well ; then he became a librarian in a
private library, tried various other professions, and

at length, having passed an attorney's examination, he began drinking, and came across the captain. He was a bald-headed man, with a stoop, and a sharp-pointed nose. In a thin, yellow face, with a pointed beard, glittered restless, sad, deep-sunk eyes, and the corners of his mouth were drawn down, giving him a depressed expression. His livelihood, or rather the means to get drunk, he earned by being a reporter on the local newspapers. Sometimes he would earn as much as fifteen roubles a week; these he would give to the captain, saying, "This is the last of it! Another week of hard work, and I shall get enough to be decently dressed, and then—*addio, mio caro !*"

"That's all right; you have my hearty approbation. I won't give you another glass of vodka the whole week," the captain would reply severely.

"I shall be very grateful. You must not give me a single drop."

The captain heard in these words something approaching very near to a humble appeal, and would add still more severely, "You may shout for it, but I won't give you any more."

"Well, that's an end of it," the teacher would sigh, and go off to his work. But in a day or two, feeling exhausted, fatigued, and thirsty, he would look furtively at the captain, with sad, imploring eyes, hoping anxiously that his friend's heart would melt. The captain would keep a severe face, uttering speeches full of the disgrace of weak natures, of the bestial pleasures of drunkenness, and other words applicable to the circumstances. To give him his due, it is right to add that he was sincere in his rôle of mentor and of moralist, but the patrons of his doss-house always inclined to be sceptical, and while listening to the scathing words of the captain, would say to each other with a wink, "He's a sly one for knowing how to get rid of all responsibility himself! 'I told you so; but you wouldn't listen to me; now blame yourself.'"

"The gentleman is an old soldier; he doesn't advance without preparing a retreat."

The schoolmaster would catch his friend in a dark corner, and holding him by his dirty cloak, trembling and moistening his parched lips with his tongue, would look into the captain's eyes with an expression so deeply tragic that no words could describe it.

"Can't you?" the captain would question sombrely.

The schoolmaster would silently nod, and then drop his head on his chest, trembling through all his long, thin body.

"Try one more day; perhaps you will conquer yourself," proposed Kouvalda.

The schoolmaster would sigh and shake his head in a hopeless negative. When the captain saw that his friend's lean body was shaken with the thirst for poison, he would take the money out of his pocket.

"It's generally useless to argue with fate," he would say, as if wishing to justify himself.

But if the schoolmaster held out the whole week, the farewell of the friends terminated in a touching scene, the end of which generally took place in Vaviloff's vodka shop.

The schoolmaster never drank all his money; at least half of it he spent on the children of the High Street. Poor people are always rich in children, and in the dust and ditches in this street might be seen from morning till night groups of torn, hungry, noisy youngsters. Children are the living flowers of the earth, but in the High Street they were like flowers faded before their time; probably because they grew on soil poor in nourishing qualities.

Sometimes the schoolmaster would gather the children round him, buy a quantity of bread, eggs, apples, nuts, and go with them into the fields towards the river. There they would greedily eat up all he had to offer them, filling the air around with merry noise and laughter. The lank, thin figure of the drunkard seemed to shrivel up and grow small like the little ones round him, who treated him with complete familiarity, as if he were one of their own age. They called him "Philippe," not adding even the title of "uncle." They jumped around him like eels, they pushed him, got on his back, slapped his bald head, and pulled his nose. He probably liked it, for he never protested against these liberties being taken. He spoke very little to them, and his words were humble and timid, as if he were afraid that his voice might soil or hurt them. He spent many hours with them, sometimes as plaything, and at other times as playmate. He used to look into their bright faces with sad eyes, and would then slowly and thoughtfully slink off into Vaviloff's vodka shop, where he would drink till he lost consciousness.

Almost every day when he returned from his reporting, the schoolmaster would bring back a paper from the town, and the outcasts would form a circle round him.   As soon as they saw him coming, they would gather from the different corners of the yard, some drunk, some in a state of stupor, all in different stages of raggedness, but all equally miserable and dirty.

First would appear Alexai Maximovitch Simtzoff, round as a barrel; formerly a surveyor of forest lands, but now a pedlar of matches, ink, blacking, and bad lemons.   He was an old man of sixty, in a canvas coat and a broad-brimmed crushed hat, which covered his fat red face, with its thick white beard, out of which peeped forth a small red nose, and thick lips of the same colour, and weak, running, cynical eyes.   They called him " Kubar," a top, and this nickname well portrayed his round, slowly moving figure and his thick, humming speech.

Louka Antonovitch Martianoff, nicknamed Konetz, " The End," would come out of some corner, a morose, black, silent drunkard, formerly an inspector of a prison; a man who gained his livelihood at present by playing games of hazard, such as the three-card trick and thimble-rig, and by the display of other talents equally ingenious, but equally unappreciated by the police.   He would drop his heavy, often ill-treated, body on the grass beside the schoolmaster, his black eyes glistening, and stretching forth his hand to the bottle, would ask in a hoarse bass voice—

" May I ? "

Then also would draw near the mechanic Pavel Sontseff, a consumptive of about thirty. The ribs on his left side had been broken in a street row; and his face, yellow and sharp, was constantly twisted into a cunning, wicked smile. His thin lips showed two rows of black, decayed teeth, and the rags on his thin shoulders seemed to be hanging on a peg. They used to call him "Scraps"; he earned his living by selling brooms of his own making, and brushes made of a certain kind of grass, which were very useful for brushing clothes.

Besides these, there was a tall, bony, one-eyed man with uncertain antecedents; he had a scared expression in his large, round, silent, and timid eyes. He had been three times condemned for thefts, and had suffered imprisonment for them. His name was Kisselnikoff, but he was nicknamed "Tarass and a half" because he was just half the size again of his inseparable friend Tarass, a former church deacon, but degraded now for drunkenness and dissipation. The deacon was a short, robust little man with a broad chest and a round, matted head of hair; he was famous for his dancing, but more so for his swearing; both he and "Tarass and a half" chose as their special work wood-sawing on the river-bank, and in their leisure hours the deacon would tell long stories "of his own composition," as he expressed it, to his friend or to anyone who cared to hear them. Whilst listening to these stories, the heroes of which were always saints, kings, clergy, and generals, even the habitués of the doss-house used to spit the taste of them out of their mouths, and opened wide eyes of astonishment at the wonderful imagination of the deacon, who would relate these shameless, obscene, fantastic adventures with great coolness, and with eyes closed in rapture. The imagination of this man was powerful and inexhaustible; he could invent and talk the whole day long, and never repeated himself. In him the world lost perhaps a great poet, and certainly a remarkable story-teller, who could put life and soul even into stones, by his foul but imaginatively powerful thought.

Besides these there was an absurd youth, who was called by Kouvalda "The Meteor." He once came to seek a night's lodging, and to the astonishment of all he never left. At first no one noticed him, for during the day he would go out to earn a livelihood, as did the rest, but in the evening he stuck closely to the friendly doss-house society. One day the captain asked him—

"My lad, what do you do in this world?"

The boy answered shortly and boldly, "I? I'm a tramp."

The captain looked at him critically. The lad had long hair, a broad, foolish face adorned with a snub nose; he wore a blue blouse without a belt, and on his head were the remains of a straw hat. His feet were bare.

"You are a fool!" said Aristide Kouvalda. "What are you doing here? You are of no use to us. Do you drink vodka? No! And can you steal? Not that either? Well, go and learn all that, and make a man of yourself, and then come back."

The lad smiled. "No, I shan't; I'll stay where I am!"

"Why?"

"Because"—

"Ah! you're a meteor!" said the captain.

"Let me knock some of his teeth out," proposed Martianoff.

"But why?" asked the lad.

"Because"—

"Well, then, I should take a stone and knock you on the head," replied the boy respectfully.

Martianoff would have thrashed him if Kouvalda had not interfered. "Leave him alone; he is distantly related to you, brother, as he is to all of us. You, without sufficient reason, want to knock his teeth out; and he, also without sufficient reason, wants to live with us. Well, damn it all! We all have to live without sufficient reason for doing so. We live, but ask us why; we can't say. Well, it's so with him, so let him be."

"But still, young man, you had better leave us," the schoolmaster intervened, surveying the lad with sad eyes.

The lad did not answer, but remained. At last they grew accustomed to him, and paid no attention to him, but he watched closely all that they said and did.

All the above-mentioned individuals formed the captain's bodyguard, and with good-natured irony he used to call them his "Outcasts." Besides these, there were five or six tramp rank-and-file in the doss-house; these were country-folk who could not boast of such antecedents as the outcasts, though they had undergone no less vicissitudes of fate; but they were a degree less degraded, and not so completely broken down. It may be that a decent man from the educated classes in town is somewhat above a decent peasant; but it is inevitable that a vicious townsman should be immeasurably more degraded in mind than a criminal from the country. This rule was strikingly illustrated by the inhabitants of Kouvalda's dwelling.

The most prominent peasant representative was a rag-picker of the name of Tiapa. Tall, and horribly thin, he constantly carried his head so that his chin fell on his breast, and from this position his shadow always assumed the shape of a hook.

One could never see his full face, but his profile showed an aquiline nose, projecting underlip, and bushy grey eyebrows. He was the captain's first lodger, and it was rumoured that he possessed large sums of money hidden somewhere about him. It was for this money that two years ago he had had his throat cut, since when he had been forced to keep his head so strangely bent. He denied having any money, and said that he had been struck with a knife for fun; and this accident had made it convenient for him to become a rag and bone picker, as his head was always necessarily bent forward towards the ground. When he walked about with his swaying, uncertain gait, and without his stick and bag, the badges of his profession, he seemed a being absorbed with his own thoughts, and Kouvalda, pointing at him with his finger, would say, " Look out ! there is the escaped conscience of Judah Petounnikoff, seeking for a refuge ! See how ragged and dirty this fugitive conscience looks ! "

Tiapa spoke with such a hoarse voice that it was almost impossible to understand him, and that was perhaps why he spoke little, and always sought solitude. Each time, when a new-comer, driven from the village, arrived at the doss-house, Tiapa at sight of him would fall into a state of angry irritation and restlessness. He would persecute the miserable being with sharp, mocking words, which issued from his throat in an angry hiss ; and he would set on him one of the most savage amongst the tramps, and finally threaten to beat and rob him himself in the night. He nearly always succeeded in driving out the terrified and disconcerted peasant, who never returned.

When Tiapa was somewhat appeased, he would hide himself in a corner to mend his old clothes or to read in a Bible, as old, as torn, as dirty as himself. Tiapa would come out of his corner when the schoolmaster brought the newspaper to read. Generally Tiapa listened silently to the news, sighed deeply, but never asked any questions. When the schoolmaster closed the newspaper, Tiapa would stretch out his bony hand and say—

" Give it here."

" What do you want it for ? "

" Give it ; perhaps there is something written concerning us."

" Concerning whom ? "

" The village."

They laughed at him, and threw the paper at him. He would take it and read those parts which told of corn beaten down by the hail; of thirty holdings being destroyed by fire, and of a woman poisoning a whole family; in fact, all those parts about village life which showed it as miserable, sordid, and cruel. Tiapa read all these in a dull voice, and emitted sounds which might be interpreted as expressing either pity or pleasure. On Sunday he never went out rag-picking, but spent most of his day reading his Bible, during which process he moaned and sighed. His book he always held resting on his chest, and he was angry if anyone touched it or interrupted his reading.

" Hullo, you magician ! " Kouvalda would say ; " you don't understand anything of that ; leave the book alone ! "

" And you ? What do you understand ? "

" Well, old magician, I don't understand anything ; but then I don't read books."

" But I do."

" More fool you ! " answered the captain. " It's bad enough to have vermin in the head. But to get thoughts into the bargain. How will you ever be able to live, you old toad ? "

" Well, I have not got much longer to live," said Tiapa quietly.

One day the schoolmaster inquired where he had learned to read, and Tiapa answered shortly—

" In prison."

" Have you been there ? "

" Yes, I have."

" For what ? "

" Because—I made a mistake. It was there I got my Bible. A lady gave it me. It's good in prison, don't you know that, brother ? "

" It can't be. What is there good in it ? "

" They teach one there. You see how I was taught to read. They gave me a book, and all that free ! "

When the schoolmaster came to the doss-house, Tiapa had been there already a long time. He watched the schoolmaster constantly ; he would bend his body on one side in order to get a good look at him, and would listen attentively to his conversation.

Once he began, " Well, I see you are a learned man. Have you ever read the Bible ? "

" Yes, I have."

" Well, do you remember it ? "

" I do ! What then ? "

The old man bent his whole body on one side and looked at the schoolmaster with grey, morose, distrustful eyes.

" And do you remember anything about the Amalekites ? "

" Well, what then ? "

" Where are they now ? "

" They have died out, Tiapa—disappeared."

The old man was silent, but soon he asked again—

" And the Philistines ? "

" They've gone also."

" Have they all disappeared ? "

" Yes, all."

" Does that mean that we shall also disappear as well ? "

" Yes, when the time comes," the schoolmaster replied, in an indifferent tone of voice.

" And to which tribe of Israel do we belong ? "

The schoolmaster looked at him steadily, thought for a moment, and began telling him about the Cymri, the Scythians, the Huns, and the Slavs.

The old man seemed to bend more than ever on one side, and watched the schoolmaster with scared eyes.

" You are telling lies ! " he hissed out, when the schoolmaster had finished.

" Why do you think I am lying ? " asked the astonished schoolmaster.

" Those people you have spoken of, none of them are in the Bible ! " He rose and went out, deeply insulted, and cursing angrily.

" You are going mad, Tiapa ! " cried the schoolmaster after him.

Then the old man turned round, and stretching out his hand shook with a threatening action his dirty, crooked forefinger.

" Adam came from the Lord. The Jews came from Adam. And all people come from the Jews —we amongst them."

" Well ? "

" The Tartars came from Ishmael. And he came from a Jew ! "

" Well, what then ? "

"Nothing.   Only why do you tell lies?"

And he went off, leaving his companion in a state
of bewilderment.   But in two or three days' time he
approached him again.

"As you are a learned man, you ought at least to
know who we are!"

"Slavs, Tiapa—Slavs!" replied the schoolmaster.

And he awaited with interest Tiapa's answer,
hoping to understand him.

"Speak according to the Bible!   There are no
names like that in the Bible.   Who are we,
Babylonians or Edomites?"

The teacher began criticising the Bible.   The old
man listened long and attentively, and finally interrupted him.

"Stop all that!   Do you mean that among all
the people known to God there were no Russians?
We were unknown to God?   Is that what you
mean to say?   Those people, written about in the
Bible, God knew them all.   He used to punish them
with fire and sword; He destroyed their towns and
villages, but still He sent them His prophets to
teach them, which meant He loved them.   He
dispersed the Jews and Tartars, but He still pre-
served them.   And what about us?   Why have we
no prophets?"

"Well, I don't know," said the schoolmaster,
trying in vain to understand the old man.

The old peasant put his hand on the schoolmaster's shoulder, rocking him gently to and fro
whilst he hissed and gurgled as if swallowing something, and muttered in a hoarse voice—

" You should have said so long ago. And you went on talking as if you knew everything. It makes me sick to hear you. It troubles my soul. You'd better hold your tongue. See, you don't even know why we have no prophets. You don't know where we were when Jesus was on earth. And such lies too. Can a whole people die out? The Russian nation can't disappear; it's all lies. They are mentioned somewhere in the Bible, only I don't know under what name. Don't you know what a nation means? It is immense. See how many villages there are! And in each village look at the number of people; and you say they will die out. A people cannot die out, but a person can. A people is necessary to God, for they till the soil. The Amalekites have not died out; they are the French or the Germans. And see what you have been telling me. You ought to know why we don't possess God's favour; He never sends us now either plagues or prophets. So how *can* we be taught now ? "

Tiapa's speech was terribly powerful. It was penetrated with irony, reproach, and fervent faith. He spoke for a long time, and the schoolmaster, who was as usual half drunk, and in a peaceful frame of mind, got tired of listening. He felt as if his nerves were being sawn with a wooden saw. He was watching the distorted body of the old man, and feeling the strange oppressive strength in his words. Finally he fell to pitying himself, and from that passed into a sad, wearied mood. He also wanted to say something forcible to old Tiapa, something positive, that might win the old man's favour, and change his reproachful, morose tone into one that was soft and fatherly. The schoolmaster felt as if words were rising to his lips, but could not find any strong enough to express his thought.

"Ah! You are a lost man," said Tiapa. "Your soul is torn, and yet you speak all sorts of empty fine words. You'd better be silent!"

"Ah, Tiapa!" sadly exclaimed the schoolmaster, "all that you say is true. And about the people also. The mass of the people is immense! But I am a stranger to it, and it is a stranger to me. There lies the tragedy of my life! But what's to be done? I must go on suffering. Indeed there are no prophets; no, not any. And it's true I talk too much and to no purpose. I had better hold my tongue. But you mustn't be so hard on me. Ah, old man, you don't know! You don't know. You can't understand."

Finally the schoolmaster burst into tears; he cried so easily and freely, with such abundant tears, that afterwards he felt quite relieved.

"You should go into the country; you should get a place as schoolmaster or as clerk. You would be comfortable there, and have a change of air. What's the use of leading this miserable life here?" Tiapa hissed morosely.

But the schoolmaster continued to weep, enjoying his tears.

From that time forth they became friends, and the outcasts, seeing them together, would say—

" The schoolmaster is making up to old Tiapa ; he is trying to get at his money."

" It's Kouvalda who has put him up to trying to find out where the old man's hoard is."

It is very possible that their words were not in agreement with their thoughts ; for these people had one strange trait in common—they liked to appear to each other worse than they really were.

The man who has nothing good in him likes sometimes to show himself in the worst light.

When all of them were gathered round the schoolmaster with his newspaper, the reading would begin.

" Now," would say the captain, " what does the paper offer us to-day ? Is there a serial story coming out in it ? "

" No," the schoolmaster would reply.

" Your editor is mean. Is there a leading article ? "

" Yes, there is one to-day. I think it is by Gouliaff."

" Give us a taste of it ! The fellow writes well. He's a cute one, he is ! "

" The valuation of real estate," reads the school-master, " which took place more than fifteen years ago, continues still to form a basis for present-day rating, to the great advantage of the town."

" The rogues ! " interjects Captain Kouvalda. " ' Still continues to form ! ' It's indeed absurd ! It's to the advantage of the merchants who manage the affairs of the town that it should continue to form the basis, and that's why it does continue ! "

"Well, the article is written with that idea," says the schoolmaster.

"Ah! is it? How strange! It would be a good theme for the serial story, where it could be given a spicy flavour!"

A short dispute arises. The company still listens attentively, for they are at their first bottle of vodka. After the leading article they take the local news. After that they attack the police news, and law cases. If in these a merchant is the sufferer, Aristide Kouvalda rejoices. If a merchant is robbed, all is well; it is only a pity they did not take more. If his horses ran away with him and smashed him up, it was pleasant to listen to, and only a pity that the fellow escaped alive. If a shopkeeper lost a lawsuit, that was a good hearing; the sad point was that he was not made to pay the expenses twice over.

"That would have been illegal," remarks the schoolmaster.

"Illegal?" Kouvalda exclaims hotly. "But does a shopkeeper himself act always according to the law? What is a shopkeeper? Let us examine this vulgar, absurd creature. To begin with, every shopkeeper is a moujik. He comes from the country, and after a certain time he takes a shop and begins to trade. To keep a shop one must have money, and where can a moujik or peasant get money? As everyone knows, money is not earned by honest labour. It means that the peasant by some means or other has cheated. It means that a shopkeeper is a dishonest peasant!"

"That's clever!" The audience shows its approbation of the orator's reasoning.

Tiapa groans and rubs his chest; the sound is like that which he makes after swallowing his first glass of vodka.

The captain is buoyant. They now begin reading provincial correspondence. Here the captain is in his own sphere, as he expresses it. Here it is apparent how shamefully the shopkeeper lives, and how he destroys and disfigures life. Kouvalda's speech thunders round the shopkeeper, and annihilates him. He is listened to with pleasure, for he uses violent words.

"Oh, if I could only write in newspapers!" he exclaims, "I'd show the shopkeeper up in his right colours! I'd show he was only an animal who was temporarily performing the duties of man. I can see through him very well! I know him. He's a coarse fool with no taste for life, who has no notion of patriotism, and understands nothing beyond kopecks!"

"Scraps," knowing the weak side of the captain, and delighting in arousing anger, would interpose—

"Yes, since the gentry are dying out from hunger, there is no one of any account left in the world."

"You are right, you son of a spider and of a frog! Since the gentry have gone under no one is left. There are nothing but shopkeepers, and I hate them!"

"That's easy to see; for have they not trodden you under foot?"

"What's that to me? I came down in the world

through my love of life, while the shopkeeper does not understand living. That's just why I hate him so, and not because I am a gentleman. But just take this as said, that I'm no longer a gentleman, but just simply an outcast, the shadow only of my former self. I spit at all and everything, and life for me is like a mistress who has deserted me. That is why I despise it, and am perfectly indifferent towards it."

" All lies ! " says " Scraps."

" Am I a liar ? " roars Aristide Kouvalda, red with anger.

" Why roar like that ? " says Martianoff's bass voice, coolly and gloomily. " What's the use of arguing ? Shopkeeper or gentleman, what does it matter to us ? "

" That's just it, for we are neither fish, nor fowl, nor good red herring," interposes Deacon Tarass.

" Leave him in peace, ' Scraps,' " says the schoolmaster pacifically. " What's the use of throwing oil on the fire ? "

The schoolmaster did not like quarrels and noise. When passions grew hot around him his lips twitched painfully, and he unobtrusively tried to make peace ; not succeeding in which, he would leave the company to themselves. The captain knew this well, and if he was not very drunk he restrained himself, not wishing to lose the best auditor of his brilliant speeches.

" I repeat," he continued now, with more restraint —" I repeat, that I see that life is in the hands of foes, not only of foes of the nobility, but foes of all that is noble; of greedy, ignorant people, who won't do anything to improve the conditions of life.   Still," argues the schoolmaster, "merchants created Genoa, Venice, Holland.   It was the merchants, the merchants of England who won India.   It was the merchants Stroganoffs "—

"What have I to do with those merchants?   I am speaking of Judah Petounnikoff and his kind, with whom I have to do."

"And what have you to do with these?" asked the schoolmaster softly.

"Well, I'm alive.   I'm in the world.   I can't help being indignant at the thought of these savages, who have got hold of life, and who are doing their best to spoil it!"

"And who are laughing at the noble indignation of a captain and an outcast!" interjects "Scraps" provokingly.

"It's stupid, very stupid!   I agree with you. As an outcast I must destroy all the feelings and thoughts that were once in me.   That's perhaps true; but how shall we arm ourselves, you and I, if we throw on one side these feelings?"

"Now you are beginning to speak reasonably," says the schoolmaster encouragingly.

"We want something different.   New ways of looking at life, new feelings, something fresh, for we ourselves are a new phase in life."

"Yes, indeed, that's what we want," says the schoolmaster.

"What's the use of discussing and thinking?" inquires "The End"; "we haven't got long to live;

I'm forty, you are fifty. There is no one under thirty among us. And even if one were twenty, one could not live very long in such surroundings as these."

"And then again, what new phase are we? Tramps, it seems to me, have always existed in the world," says "Scraps" satirically.

"Tramps created Rome," says the schoolmaster.

"Yes; that was so!" said the captain jubilantly. "Romulus and Remus, were they not tramps? And we—when our time comes—we shall also create."

"A breach of the peace!" interjects "Scraps," and laughs, pleased with his own wit.

His laugh is wicked, and jars on the nerves. He is echoed by Simtzoff, by the deacon, and by "Tarass and a half." The naïve eyes of the lad "Meteor" burn with a bright glow, and his cheeks flush red. "The End" mutters, in tones that fall like a hammer on the heads of the audience—

"All that's trash and nonsense, and dreams!"

It was strange to hear these people, outcasts from life, ragged, saturated with vodka, anger, irony, and filth, discussing life in this way.

For the captain such discussions were a feast. He spoke more than the others, and that gave him a chance of feeling his superiority. For however low a person may fall, he can never refuse himself the delight of feeling stronger and better off than the rest. Aristide Kouvalda abused this sensation, and never seemed to have enough of it, much to the disgust of "Scraps," "The Top," and the other outcasts, little interested in similar questions. Poli-

tics was with them the favourite topic. A discussion
on the necessity of conquering India, and of checking
England, would continue endlessly. The question
as to the best means of sweeping the Jews off the
face of the earth, was no less hotly debated. In
this latter question the leader was always " Scraps,"
who invented marvellously cruel projects; but the
captain, who liked always to be first in a discussion,
evaded this topic. Women were always willingly
and constantly discussed, but with unpleasant allu-
sions; and the schoolmaster always appeared as
women's champion, and grew angry when the
expressions used by the others were of too strong
a nature. They gave in to him, for they looked
upon him as a superior being, and on Saturdays
they would borrow money from him, which he had
earned during the week.

He enjoyed besides many privileges. For instance, he was never knocked about on the frequent
occasions when the discussions finished in a general
row. He was allowed to bring women into the
doss-house; and no one else enjoyed this right, for
the captain always warned his clients—

" I'll have no women here ! Women, shopkeepers,
and philosophy have been the three causes of my
ruin. I'll knock down anyone I see with a woman,
and I'll knock the woman down as well. On prin-
ciple, I would twist the neck of "—

He could have twisted anyone's neck, for in
spite of his years he possessed wonderful strength.
Besides, whenever he had a fighting job on, he was
always helped by Martianoff. Gloomy and silent

as the tomb in the usual way, yet on these occasions, when there was a general row on, he would stand back to back with Kouvaloff, these two forming together a destructive but indestructible engine. If Kouvalda was engaged in a hand-to-hand fight, "The End" would creep up and throw his opponent on the ground.

Once when Simtzoff was drunk, he, without any reason, caught hold of the schoolmaster's hair and pulled a handful out. Kouvalda, with one blow of his fist, dropped Simtzoff unconscious, and he lay where he fell for half an hour. When the fellow came to his senses he was made to swallow the schoolmaster's hair, which he did for fear of being beaten to death.

Besides the reading of the newspaper, discussions, and laughter, the other amusement was card-playing. They always left Martianoff out, for he could not play honestly. After being several times caught cheating, he candidly confessed—

"I can't help cheating; it's a habit of mine."

"Such things do happen," corroborated Deacon Tarass. "I used to have the habit of beating my wife every Sunday after mass; and, would you believe it, after she died I had such a gnawing feeling come over me every Sunday I can scarcely describe it. I got over one Sunday, but things seemed to go all wrong. Another Sunday passed, and I felt very bad. The third Sunday I could not bear it any longer, and struck the servant girl. She kicked up a row, and threatened to take me before a magistrate. Just imagine my position! When the fourth Sunday came I knocked her about as I used to do my wife; I paid her ten roubles down, and arranged that I should beat her as a matter of course until I married again."

"Deacon, you are telling lies! How could you marry again?" broke in "Scraps."

"Well—I—she—we did without the ceremony. She kept house for me."

"Had you any children?" asked the school-master.

"Yes, five of them. One got drowned—the eldest. He was a queer boy. Two died of diphtheria. One daughter married a student, and followed him to Siberia. The other wanted to study in Petersburg, and died there; I am told it was consumption. Yes, five of them. We clergy are very prolific."

And he began giving reasons for this, causing by his explanations Homeric laughter. When they were tired of laughing, Alexai Maximovitch Simtzoff remembered that he also had a daughter.

"She was called Lidka. Oh, how fat she was!"

Probably he remembered nothing more, for he looked round deprecatingly, smiled, and found nothing more to say.

These people spoke but little of their past. They seldom recalled it, and if ever they did so, it was in general terms, and in a more or less scoffing tone. Perhaps they were right in treating their past slightingly, for recollections with most people have a tendency to weaken present energy, and destroy hope in the future.

On rainy days, and during dark, cold, autumn weather, these outcasts would gather in Vaviloff's vodka shop. They were habitués there, and were feared as a set of thieves and bullies; on one hand they were despised as confirmed drunkards, and on the other hand they were respected and listened to as superior people. Vaviloff's vodka shop was the club of the neighbourhood, and the outcasts were the intellectuals of the club.

On Saturday evenings, and on Sundays from early morning till night, the vodka shop was full of people, and the outcasts were welcome guests. They brought with them, amongst these inhabitants of the High Street, oppressed as they were by poverty and misery, a rollicking humour, in which there was something that seemed to brighten these lives, broken and worn out in the struggle for bread. The outcasts' art of talking jestingly on every subject, their fearlessness of opinion, their careless audacity of expression, their absence of fear of everything which the neighbourhood feared, their boldness, their dare-devilry—all this did not fail to please. Besides, almost all of them knew something of law, could give advice on many matters, could write a petition, or could give a helping hand in a shady transaction without getting into trouble. They were paid in vodka, and in flattering encomiums on their various talents.

According to their sympathies, the street was divided into two nearly equal parties. One considered that the captain was very superior to the schoolmaster: " A real hero! His pluck and his intelligence are far greater!" The other considered that the schoolmaster outbalanced Kouvalda in every respect. The admirers of Kouvalda were those who were known in the street as confirmed drunkards, thieves, and scapegraces, who feared neither poverty nor prison. The schoolmaster was admired by those who were more decent, who were always hoping for something, always expecting something, and yet whose bellies were always empty.

The respective merits of Kouvalda and the schoolmaster may be judged of by the following example. Once in the vodka shop they were discussing the town regulations under which the inhabitants of the neighbourhood were bound to fill up the ruts and holes in the streets; the dead bodies of animals and manure were not to be used for this purpose, but rubble and broken bricks from buildings.

" How the devil am I to get broken bricks? I, who all my life have been wanting to build a starling house, and yet have never been able to begin?" complained in a pitiful voice Mokei Anissimoff, a seller of kringels [1] which were made by his wife.

The captain considered that he ought to give an opinion on the question, and thumped the table energetically to attract the attention of the company.

" Don't you know where to get bricks and rubble? Let's go all of us, my lads, into the town together and demolish the Town Hall. It's an old, good-for-nothing building, and your work will be crowned

[1] A sort of white bread of a particular shape, which is very popular amongst the Russian peasantry.

by a double success. You will improve the town by
forcing them to build a new Town Hall, and you
will make your own neighbourhood decent. You
can use the Mayor's horses to draw the bricks, and
you can take his three daughters as well; the girls
would look well in harness! Or else you may pull
down Judah Petounnikoff's house, and mend the
street with wood. By the bye, Mokei, I know what
your wife was using to-day to heat the oven for
baking her kringels! It was the shutters from the
third window, and the boards from two of the
steps!"

When the audience had had its laugh out, and
had finished joking at the captain's proposal, the
serious-minded gardener Pavluguine asked—

"But, after all, captain, what's to be done?
What do you advise us to do?"

"I—I advise you not to move hand or foot. If
the rain destroys the street, let it. It isn't our
fault."

"Some of the houses are tumbling down already."

"Leave them alone, let them fall! If they come
down the town must pay damages, and if the
authorities refuse, bring the matter before a magistrate. For just consider where the water comes
from; doesn't it come down from the town? Well,
that shows the town is to blame for the houses
being destroyed."

"They will say it's rain water."

"But in the town the rain doesn't wash down
the houses, does it? The town makes you pay
rates and gives you no vote to help you claim your

rights. The town destroys your life and your property, and yet holds you responsible for them. Pitch into the town on every side!"

And one half of the dwellers in the street, convinced by the radical Kouvalda, decided to wait till the storm-waters of the town had washed down their hovels.

The more serious half got the schoolmaster to write out an elaborate, convincing report for presentation to the town authorities. In this report, the refusal to carry out the town regulations was based on such solid reasons that the municipality was bound to take them into consideration. The dwellers in the street were granted permission to use the refuse left after the rebuilding of the barracks, and five horses from the fire brigade were lent to cart the rubbish. Besides this it was decided to lay a drain down the street.

This, added to other circumstances, made the schoolmaster very popular in the neighbourhood. He wrote petitions, got articles put into the papers. Once, for instance, the guests at Vaviloff's noticed that the herrings and other coarse food were not up to the mark, and two days later Vaviloff, standing at the counter with the newspaper in his hands, made a public recantation.

" It's quite just. I have nothing to say for myself. The herrings were indeed rotten when I bought them, and the cabbage—that's also true— had been lying about too long. Well, it's only natural everyone wants to put more kopecks into his own pocket. And what comes of it? Just the opposite to what one hopes. I tried to get at other men's pockets, and a clever man has shown me up for my avarice. Now we're quits!"

This recantation produced an excellent effect on his audience, and gave Vaviloff the chance of using up all his bad herrings and stale cabbage, the public swallowing them down unheeding their ancient flavour, which was concealed with the spice of a favourable impression. This event was remarkable in two ways; it not only increased the prestige of the schoolmaster, but it taught the inhabitants the value of the Press.

Sometimes the schoolmaster would hold forth on practical morality.

"I saw," he would say, accosting the house painter Jashka Turine, "I saw, Jakoff, how you were beating your wife to-day."

Jashka had already raised his spirits with two glasses of vodka, and was in a jovial mood. The company looked at him, expecting some sally, and silence reigned in the vodka shop.

"Well, if you saw it I hope you liked it!" said Jashka.

The company laughed discreetly.

"No, I didn't like it," answered the schoolmaster; his tone of voice was suggestively serious, and silence fell on the listeners.

"I did what I could; in fact I tried to do my best," said Jashka, trying to brave it out, but feeling he was about to catch it from the schoolmaster. "My wife has had enough; she won't be able to get out of bed to-day."

The schoolmaster traced with his forefinger some figures on the table, and whilst examining them said—

"Look here, Jakoff, this is why I don't like it. Let us go thoroughly into the question of what you are doing, and of what may be the result of it. Your wife is with child; you beat her yesterday all over the body; you might, when you do that, kill the child, and when your wife is in labour she might die or be seriously ill. The trouble of having a sick wife is not pleasant; it may cost you also a good deal, for illness means medicine, and medicine means money. If, even, you are fortunate enough not to have killed the child, you have certainly injured it, and it will very likely be born hunch-backed or crooked, and that means it won't be fit for work. It is of importance to you that the child should be able to earn its living. Even supposing it is only born delicate, that also will be an awkward business for you. It will be a burden to its mother, and it will require care and medicine. Do you see what you are laying up in store for yourself? Those who have to earn their living must be born healthy and bear healthy children. Am I not right?"

"Quite right," affirms the company.

"But let's hope this won't happen," says Jashka, rather taken aback by the picture drawn by the schoolmaster. "She's so strong one can't touch the child through her. Besides, what's to be done? she's such a devil. She nags and nags at me for the least trifle."

"I understand, Jakoff, that you can't resist

beating your wife," continued the schoolmaster, in his quiet, thoughtful voice. "You may have many reasons for it, but it's not your wife's temper that causes you to beat her so unwisely. The cause is your unenlightened and miserable condition."

"That's just so," exclaimed Jakoff. "We do indeed live in darkness—in darkness as black as pitch!"

"The conditions of your life irritate you, and your wife has to suffer for it. She is the one nearest to you in the world, and she is the innocent sufferer just because you are the stronger of the two. She is always there ready to your hand; she can't get away from you. Don't you see how absurd it is of you?"

"That's all right, damn her! But what am I to do? Am I not a man?"

"Just so; you are a man. Well, don't you see what I want to explain to you? If you must beat her, do so; but beat her carefully. Remember that you can injure her health and that of the child. Remember, as a general rule, it is bad to beat a woman who is with child on the breasts, or the lower part of the body. Beat her on the back of the neck, or take a rope and strike her on the fleshy parts of the body."

As the orator finished his speech, his sunken dark eyes glanced at the audience as if asking pardon or begging for something. The audience was in a lively, talkative mood. This morality of an outcast was to it perfectly intelligible — the morality of the vodka shop and of poverty.

" Well, brother Jashka, have you understood ? "

" Damn it all ! there's truth in what you say."

Jakoff understood one thing—that to beat his wife unwisely might be prejudicial to himself.

He kept silence, answering his friends' jokes with shamefaced smiles.

" And then again, look what a wife can be to one," philosophises the kringel - seller, Mokei Anissimoff. " One's wife is a friend, if you look at the matter in the right light. She is, as it were, chained to one for life, like a fellow-convict, and one must try and walk in step with her. If one gets out of step, the chain galls."

" Stop ! " says Jakoff. " You beat your wife also, don't you ? "

" I'm not saying I don't, because I do. How can I help it ? I can't beat the wall with my fists when I feel I must beat something ! "

" That's just how I feel," says Jakoff.

" What an existence is ours, brothers ! So narrow and stifling, one can never have a real fling."

" One has even to beat one's wife with caution," humorously condoles someone.

Thus they would go on gossiping late into the night, or until a row would begin, provoked by their state of drunkenness, or by the impressions aroused by these conversations.

Outside the rain beats against the window and the icy wind howls wildly. Inside the air is close, heavy with smoke, but warm. In the street it is wet, cold, and dark ; the gusts of wind seem to strike insolently against the window panes as if

inviting the company to go outside, and threatening
to drive them like dust over the face of the earth.
Now and then is heard in its howling a suppressed
moan, followed at intervals by what sounds like a
hoarse, chill laugh. These sounds suggest sad
thoughts of coming winter; of the damp, short,
sunless days, and of the long nights; of the necessity
for providing warm clothes and much food. There
is little sleep to be got during these long winter
nights if one has an empty stomach! Winter is
coming—is coming! How is one to live through it?

These sad thoughts encouraged thirst among the
dwellers in the High Street, and the sighs of the
outcasts increased the number of wrinkles on their
foreheads. Their voices sounded more hollow, and
their dull, slow thought kept them, as it were, at a
distance from each other. Suddenly amongst them
there flashed forth anger like that of wild beasts or
the desperation of those who are overdriven and
crushed down by a cruel fate, or else they seemed to
feel the proximity of that unrelenting foe who had
twisted and contorted their lives into one long, cruel
absurdity. But this foe was invulnerable because he
was unknown.

Then they took to beating one another, and they
struck each other cruelly, wildly. After making it
up again they would fall to drinking once more, and
drink till they had pawned everything that the easy-
going Vaviloff would accept as a pledge.

Thus, in dull anger, in trouble that crushed the
heart, in the uncertainty of the issue of this miserable
existence, they spent the autumn days awaiting the

still harder days of winter.   During hard times like these Kouvalda would come to their rescue with his philosophy.

"Pluck up courage, lads!   All comes to an end! —that's what there is best about life!   Winter will pass and summer will follow; good times when, as they say, 'even a sparrow has beer'!"

But his speeches were of little avail; a mouthful of pure water does not satisfy a hungry stomach.

Deacon Tarass would also try to amuse the company by singing songs and telling stories.   He had more success.   Sometimes his efforts would suddenly arouse desperate, wild gaiety in the vodka shop.   They would sing, dance, shout with laughter, and for some hours would behave like maniacs.   And then—

And then they would fall into a dull, indifferent state of despair as they sat round the gin-shop table in the smoke of the lamps and the reek of tobacco; gloomy, ragged, letting words drop idly from their lips while they listened to the triumphant howl of the wind; one thought uppermost in their minds—how to get more vodka to drown their senses and to bring unconsciousness.   And each of them hated the other with a deadly, senseless hatred, but hid that hatred deep down in his heart.

II

Everything in this world is relative, and there is no situation which cannot be matched with a worse one.

One fine day at the end of September Captain
Kouvalda sat, as was his custom, in his arm-chair at
the door of the doss-house looking at the big brick
building erected by the merchant Petounnikoff by
the side of Vaviloff's vodka shop. Kouvalda was
deep in thought.

This building, from which the scaffolding had not
yet been removed, was destined to be a candle
factory; and for some time it had been a thorn in
the captain's side, with its row of dark, empty, hollow
windows and its network of wood surrounding it
from foundation to roof. Blood-red in colour, it
resembled some cruel piece of machinery, not yet put
into motion, but which had already opened its row
of deep, greedy jaws ready to seize and gulp down
everything that came in its way. The grey, wooden
vodka shop of Vaviloff, with its crooked roof overgrown with moss, leaned up against one of the brick
walls of the factory, giving the effect of a great
parasite drawing its nourishment from it. The
captain's mind was occupied by the thought that the
old house would soon be replaced by a new one and
the doss-house would be pulled down. He would
have to seek another shelter, and it was doubtful if
he would find one as cheap and as convenient. It
was hard to be driven from a place one was used to,
and harder still because a damned shopkeeper takes
it into his head to want to make candles and soap.
And the captain felt that if he had the chance of
spoiling the game of this enemy of his he would do
it with the greatest pleasure.

Yesterday, the shopkeeper, Ivan Andreevitch

Petounnikoff, was in the yard of the doss-house with his son and an architect. They made a survey of the yard and stuck in pegs all over the place, which, after Petounnikoff had left, the captain ordered " The Meteor " to pull up and throw away.

The shopkeeper was for ever before the captain's eyes—short, lean, shrivelled up, dressed in a long garment something between an overcoat and a kaftan, with a velvet cap on his head, and wearing long, brightly polished boots. With prominent cheek-bones and a grey, sharp-pointed beard; a high, wrinkled forehead, from under which peeped narrow, grey, half-closed, watchful eyes; a hooked, gristly nose and thin-lipped mouth—taken altogether, the merchant gave the impression of being piously rapacious and venerably wicked.

" Damned offspring of a fox and a sow ! " said the captain angrily to himself, as he recalled some words of Petounnikoff's.

The merchant had come with a member of the town council to look at the house, and at the sight of the captain he had asked his companion in the abrupt dialect of Kostroma—

" Is that your tenant—that lunatic at large ? "

And since that time, more than eighteen months ago, they had rivalled each other in the art of insult.

Yesterday again there had been a slight interchange of " holy words," as the captain called his conversations with the merchant. After having seen the architect off, Petounnikoff approached the captain.

"What, still sitting—always sitting?" asked he, touching the peak of his cap in a way that left it uncertain whether he were fixing it on his head or bowing.

"And you—you are still on the prowl," echoed the captain, jerking out his lower jaw and making his beard wag in a way that might be taken for a bow by anyone not too exacting in these matters; it might also have been interpreted as the act of removing his pipe from one corner of his mouth to the other.

"I've plenty of money; that's why I'm always on the go. Money needs putting out, so I'm obliged to keep it moving," says the shopkeeper in an aggravating voice to the other, screwing up his eyes slyly.

"Which means that you are the slave of money, and not money your slave," replies Kouvalda, resisting an intense desire to kick his enemy in the stomach.

"It's all the same either way where money is concerned. But if you have no money!"—and the shopkeeper looked at the captain with bold but feigned compassion, while his trembling upper lip showed large, wolfish teeth.

"Anyone with a head on his shoulders and with a good conscience can do without it. Money generally comes when the conscience begins to grow a little out-at-elbows. The less honesty the more money!"

"That's true, but there are some people who have neither honesty nor money."

4

" That describes you when you were young, no doubt," said Kouvalda innocently.

Petounnikoff wrinkles his nose, he sighs, closes his narrow eyes, and says, " Ah ! when I was young, what heavy burdens I had to bear ! "

" Yes, I should think so ! "

" I worked ! Oh, how I worked ! "

" Yes, you worked at outwitting others ! "

" People like you and the nobility—what does it matter ? Many of them have, thanks to me. learnt to extend the hand in Christ's name."

" Ah ! then you did not assassinate, you only robbed ? " interrupted the captain.

Petounnikoff turns a sickly green and thinks it is time to change the conversation.

" You are not an over polite host; you remain sitting while your visitor stands."

" Well, he can sit down."

" There is nothing to sit on."

" There is the ground. The ground never rejects any filth ! "

" You prove that rule, but I had better leave you, you blackguard ! " says Petounnikoff coolly, though his eyes dart cold venom at the captain.

He went off leaving Kouvalda with the agreeable sensation that the merchant was afraid of him. If it were not so he would have turned him out of the doss-house long ago. It was not for the five roubles a month that the Jew let him remain on ! . . . And the captain watches with pleasure the slowly retreating back of Petounnikoff, as he walks slowly away. Kouvalda's eyes still follow the

merchant as he climbs up and down the scaffolding of his new building. He feels an intense desire
that the merchant should fall and break his back.
How many times has he not conjured up results
of this imaginary fall, as he has sat watching
Petounnikoff crawling about the scaffolding of his
new factory, like a spider crawling about its net.
Yesterday he had even imagined that one of the
boards had given way under the weight of the
merchant; and Kouvalda had jumped out of his
seat with excitement—but nothing had come of it.

And to-day, as always, before the eyes of Aristide
Kouvalda stands the great red building, so four-
square, so solid, so firmly fixed into the ground, as
if already drawing from thence its nourishment.
It seemed as if mocking the captain through the
cold dark yawning openings in its walls. And
the sun poured on its autumn rays with the same
prodigality as on the distorted tumble-down little
houses of the neighbourhood.

"But what if?" exclaimed the captain to himself, measuring with his eye the factory wall.
"What if?"

Aroused and excited by the thought which had
come into his mind, Aristide Kouvalda jumped up
and hastened over to Vaviloff's vodka shop, smiling,
and muttering something to himself. Vaviloff met
him at the counter with a friendly exclamation:
"How is your Excellency this morning?"

Vaviloff was a man of medium height, with a
bald head surrounded by a fringe of grey hair;
with clean-shaved cheeks, and moustache bristly as

a toothbrush. Upright and active, in a dirty braided jacket, every movement betrayed the old soldier, the former non-commissioned officer.

" Jegor! Have you the deeds and the plan of your house and property?" Kouvalda asked hastily.

" Yes, I have."

And Vaviloff closed his suspicious thievish eyes and scrutinised the captain's face, in which he observed something out of the common.

" Just show them to me!" exclaimed the captain, thumping on the counter with his fist, and dropping on to a stool.

" What for?" asked Vaviloff, who decided, in view of the captain's state of excitement, to be on his guard.

" You fool! Bring them at once!"

Vaviloff wrinkled his forehead, and looked up inquiringly at the ceiling.

" By the bye, where the devil are those papers?"

Not finding any information on this question on the ceiling, the old soldier dropped his eyes towards the ground, and began thoughtfully drumming with his fingers on the counter.

" Stop those antics!" shouted Kouvalda, who had no love for the old soldier; as, according to the captain, it was better for a former non-commissioned officer to be a thief than a keeper of a vodka shop.

" Well now, Aristide Kouvalda, I think I re-member! I believe those papers were left at the law-courts at the time when "—

" Jegorka! stop this fooling. It's to your own interest to do so. Show me the plans, the deed of sale, and all that you have got at once! Perhaps you will gain by this more than a hundred roubles! Do you understand now?"

Vaviloff understood nothing; but the captain spoke in such an authoritative and serious tone that the eyes of the old soldier sparkled with intense curiosity; and saying that he would go and see if the papers were not in his strong box, he disappeared behind the door of the counter. In a few moments he returned with the papers in his hand, and a look of great surprise on his coarse face.

"Just see! The damned things were after all in the house!"

"You circus clown! Who would think you had been a soldier!"

Kouvalda could not resist trying to shame him, whilst snatching from his hands the cotton case containing the blue legal paper. Then he spread the papers out before him, thus exciting more and more the curiosity of Vaviloff, and began reading and scrutinising them; uttering from time to time interjections in a meaning tone. Finally, he rose with an air of decision, went to the door leaving the papers on the counter, shouting out to Vaviloff—

"Wait a moment! Don't put them away yet!"

Vaviloff gathered up the papers, put them in his cash box, locked it, felt to see that it was securely fastened. Then rubbing his bald head, he went and stood in the doorway of his shop. There he saw the captain measuring with his stride the length of the front of the vodka shop, whilst he snapped his fingers from time to time, and once more began his measurements—anxious but satisfied.

Vaviloff's face wore at first a worried expression; then it grew long, and at last it suddenly beamed with joy.

"'Ristide Fomitch! Is it possible?" he exclaimed, as the captain drew near.

"Of course it's possible! More than a yard has been taken off! That's only as far as the frontage is concerned; as to the depth, I will see about that now!"

"The depth is thirty-two yards!"

"Well, I see you've guessed what I'm after. You stupid fool!"

"Well, you're a wonder, 'Ristide Fomitch! You've an eye that sees two yards into the ground!" exclaimed the delighted Vaviloff. A few minutes later they were seated opposite each other in Vaviloff's room, and the captain was swallowing great gulps of beer, and saying to the landlord—

"You see, therefore, all the factory wall stands on your ground. Act without mercy. When the schoolmaster comes we will draw up a report for the law-courts. We will reckon the damages at a moderate figure, so that the revenue stamps shan't cost us too much, but we will ask that the wall shall be pulled down. This sort of thing, you fool, is called a violation of boundaries, and it's a stroke of luck for you! To pull a great wall like that down and move it farther back is not such an easy business, and costs no end of money. Now's your chance for squeezing Judah! We will make a calculation of what the pulling down will cost, taking into consideration the value of the broken bricks and the cost of digging out the new foundations. We will calculate everything, even the value of the time, and then, O just Judah, what do you say to two thousand roubles ? "

" He won't give it ! " exclaimed Vaviloff anxiously, blinking his eyes, which were sparkling with greedy fire.

" Let him try and get out of it ! Just look, what can he do ? There will be nothing for him but to pull it down. But look out, Jegor ! Don't let yourself be worsted in the bargain. They will try and buy you off ! Mind you don't let them off too easily ! They will try and frighten you ; don't you be afraid ; rely on us to back you up ! "

The captain's eyes burnt with wild delight, and his face, purple with excitement, twitched nervously. He had succeeded in arousing the greed of the gin-shop keeper, and after having persuaded him to commence proceedings as soon as possible, went off triumphant, and implacably revengeful.

That evening all the outcasts learnt the discovery that the captain had made, and discussed eagerly the future proceedings of Petounnikoff, representing to themselves vividly his astonishment and anger the day when he should have the copy of the lawsuit presented to him. The captain was the hero of the day. He was happy, and all around were pleased. A heap of dark tattered figures lay about in the yard, talking noisily and eagerly, animated by the important event. All knew Petounnikoff, who often passed near them, blinking his eyes disdainfully, and paying as little attention to them as he did to the

rest of the rubbish lying about in the yard.   He was
a picture of self-satisfaction, and this irritated them ;
even his boots seemed to shine disdainfully at them.
But now the shopkeeper's pocket and his self-esteem
were going to be hurt by one of themselves !
Wasn't that an excellent joke ?

Evil had a singular attraction for these people ;
it was the only weapon which came easily to their
hands, and which was within their reach.   For a
long time now, each of them had cultivated within
himself dim half-conscious feelings of keen hatred
against all who, unlike themselves, were neither
hungry nor ragged.   This was why all the outcasts
felt such an intense interest in the war declared by
Kouvalda against the shopkeeper Petounnikoff.   Two
whole weeks the dwellers in the doss-house had been
living on the expectation of new developments, and
during all that time Petounnikoff did not once come
to visit the almost completed building.   They assured
each other that he was out of town, and that the
summons had not therefore yet been served upon
him.   Kouvalda raged against the delays of civil
procedure.   It is doubtful if anyone ever awaited
the arrival of the shopkeeper so impatiently as did
these tramps.

> "He comes not, he comes not !
> Alas ! he loves me not !"

sang the Deacon Tarass, leaning his chin on his
hand, and gazing with a comically sad expression up
the hill.

But one fine day, towards evening, Petounnikoff
appeared.   He arrived in a strong light cart, driven

by his son, a young man with red cheeks and wearing a long checked overcoat, and smoked blue spectacles. They tied up the horse; the son drew from his pocket a tape measure, gave one end of it to his father, and both of them silently, and with anxious expressions, began measuring the ground.

"Ah!" exclaimed triumphantly the captain.

All who were about the doss-house went and stood outside the gate watching the proceedings and expressing aloud their opinions on what was going forward.

"See what it is to have the habit of stealing! A man steals unconsciously, not intending to steal, and thereby risks more than he can gain," said the captain, with mock sympathy; thereby arousing laughter among his bodyguard, and provoking a whole string of remarks in the same strain.

"Look out, you rogue!" at length exclaimed Petounnikoff, exasperated by these jibes. "If you don't mind I'll have you up before the magistrate."

"It's of no use without witnesses, and a son can't give evidence for a father," the captain reminded him.

"All right; we shall see! Though you seem such a bold leader, you may find your match some day."

And Petounnikoff shook his forefinger at him. The son, quiet and deeply interested in his calculations, paid no heed to this group of squalid figures, who were cruelly mocking his father. He never looked once towards them.

"The young spider is well trained!" remarked

" Scraps," who was following the actions and the movements of the younger Petounnikoff.

Having taken all the necessary measurements, Ivan Andreevitch frowned, climbed silently into his cart, and drove off, whilst his son, with firm, decided steps, entered Vaviloff's vodka shop, and disappeared.

" He's a precious young thief! that he is. We shall see what comes of it!" said Kouvalda.

" What will come of it?   Why, Petounnikoff junior will square Jegor Vaviloff!" remarked " Scraps," with great assurance, smacking his lips, and with a look of keen satisfaction on his cunning face.

" That would please you, perhaps?" asked Kouvalda severely.

" It pleases me to see human calculations go wrong!" explained " Scraps," blinking his eyes and rubbing his hands.

The captain spat angrily, and kept silence. The rest of them, standing at the gate of the tumble-down house, watched silently the door of the vodka shop. An hour and more passed in this silent expectation. At length the door opened, and young Petounnikoff appeared, looking as calm as when he had entered. He paused for a moment, cleared his throat, raised his coat collar, glanced at those who were watching his movements, and turned up the street towards the town.

The captain watched him till he was out of sight, and, turning towards " Scraps," smiled ironically and said—

" It seems, after all, as if you might be right, you

son of a scorpion and of a centipede! You smell
out everything that's evil. One can see by the
dirty mug of the young rogue that he has got his
own way! I wonder how much Jegor has screwed
out of him? He's got something, that's sure!
They're birds of a feather. I'm damned if I haven't
arranged it all for them. It's cursed hard to think
what a fool I've been. You see, mates, life is dead
against us. One can't even spit into one's neighbour's face—the spittle flies back into one's own
eyes."

Consoling himself with this speech, the venerable
captain glanced at his bodyguard. All were dis-
appointed, for all felt that what had taken place
between Vaviloff and Petounnikoff had turned out
differently from what they had expected, and all
felt annoyed. The consciousness of being unable to
cause evil is more obnoxious to men than the consciousness of being unable to do good; it is so simple
and so easy to do evil!

"Well! what's the use of sticking here? We
have nothing to wait for except for Jegorka to stand
us treat," said the captain, glowering angrily at the
vodka shop. "It's all up with our peaceful and
happy life under Judah's roof. He'll send us pack-
ing now; so I give you all notice, my brigade of
sans-culottes!"

"The End" laughed morosely.

"Now then, gaoler, what's the matter with you?"
asked Kouvalda.

"Where the devil am I to go?"

"That indeed is a serious question, my friend.

But never fear, your fate will decide it for you," said the captain, turning towards the doss-house.

The outcasts followed him idly.

"We shall await the critical moment," said the captain, walking along with them. "When we get the sack there will be time enough to look out for another shelter. Meanwhile, what's the use of spoiling life with troubles like that? It is at critical moments that man rises to the occasion, and if life as a whole were to consist of nothing but critical moments, if one had to tremble every minute of one's life for the safety of one's carcass, I'll be hanged if life wouldn't be more lively, and people more interesting!"

"Which would mean that people would fly at each other's throats more savagely than they do now," explained "Scraps," smiling.

"Well, what of that?" struck in the captain, who did not care to have his ideas enlarged on.

"Nothing! nothing! It's all right—when one wants to get to one's destination quickly, one thrashes the horse, or one stokes up one's machine."

"Yes, that's it; let everything go full speed to the devil. I should be only too glad if the earth would suddenly take fire, burst up, and go to pieces, only I should like to be the last man left, to see the others."

"You're a nice one!" sneered "Scraps."

"What of that? I'm an outcast, am I not? I'm freed from all chains and fetters; therefore I can spit at everything. By the very nature of the life I lead now, I am bound to drop everything to do with the past—all fine manners and conventional ideas of people who are well fed, and well dressed, and who despise me because I am not equally well fed and dressed. So I have to cultivate in myself something fresh and new—don't you see—something you know which will make people like Judah Petounnikoff, when they pass by me, feel a cold shudder run down their backs!"

"You have a bold tongue!" sneered "Scraps."

"You miserable wretch!" Kouvalda scanned him disdainfully. "What do you understand, what do you know? You don't even know how to think! But I have thought much, I have read books of which you would not have understood a word."

"Oh, I know I'm not fit to black the boots of such a learned man! But though you have read and thought so much, and I have done neither the one nor the other, yet we are not after all so far apart."

"Go to the devil!" exclaimed Kouvalda.

His conversations with "Scraps" always finished in this way. When the schoolmaster was not about, the captain knew well that his speeches were only wasted, and were lost for want of understanding and appreciation. But for all that, he couldn't help talking, and now, having snubbed his interlocutor, he felt himself lonely amongst the others. His desire for conversation was not, however, satisfied, and he turned therefore to Simtzoff with a question.

"And you, Alexai Maximovitch, where will you lay your old head?"

The old man smiled good-naturedly, rubbed his nose with his hand, and explained—

"Don't know! Shall see by and by. I'm not of much account. A glass of vodka, that's all I want."

"A very praiseworthy ambition, and very simple," said the captain.

After a short silence Simtzoff added that he would find shelter more easily than the rest, because the women liked him.

This was true, for the old man had always two or three mistresses among the prostitutes, who would keep him sometimes for two or three days at a time on their scant earnings. They often beat him, but he took it stoically. For some reason or other they never hurt him much; perhaps they pitied him. He was a great admirer of women, but added that they were the cause of all his misfortunes in life. The close terms on which he lived with women, and the character of their relations towards him, were shown by the fact that his clothes were always neatly mended, and cleaner than the clothes of his companions. Seated now on the ground at the door of the doss-house amidst his mates, he boastfully related that he had for some time been asked by Riedka to go and live with her, but that he had till now refused, not wanting to give up the present company.

He was listened to with interest, mingled with envy. All knew Riedka; she lived not far down the hill, and only a few months ago she came out of prison after serving a second term for theft. She had formerly been a wet nurse; a tall, stout, strapping countrywoman, with a pock-marked face, and fine eyes, somewhat dulled by drink.

"The old rogue!" cursed "Scraps," watching Simtzoff, who smiled with self-satisfaction.

"And do you know why they all like me? Because I understand what their souls need."

"Indeed?" exclaimed Kouvalda interrogatively.

"I know how to make women pity me. And when a woman's pity is aroused, she can even kill, out of pure pity! Weep before her, and implore her to kill; she will have pity on you, and will kill."

"It's I who would kill!" exclaimed Martianoff, in a decided voice, with a dark scowl.

"Whom do you mean?" asked "Scraps," edging away from him.

"It's all the same to me! Petounnikoff—Jegorka —you if you like!"

"Why?" asked Kouvalda, with aroused interest.

"I want to be sent to Siberia. I'm tired of this stupid life. There one will know what to do with one's life."

"H'm!" said the captain reflectively. "You will indeed know what to do with your life there!"

Nothing more was spoken about Petounnikoff, nor of their impending expulsion from the doss-house. All were sure that this expulsion was imminent, was perhaps a matter of a few days only; and they therefore considered it useless to discuss the point further. Discussion wouldn't make it easier; besides, it was not cold yet, though the rainy season had begun. One could sleep on the ground anywhere outside the town.

Seated in a circle on the grass, they chatted idly and aimlessly, changing easily from one topic to another, and paying only just as much attention to the words of their companions as was absolutely necessary to prevent the conversation from dropping. It was a nuisance to have to be silent, but it was equally a nuisance to have to listen with attention. This society of the outcasts had one great virtue: no one ever made an effort to appear better than he was, nor forced others to try and appear better than they were.

The August sun was shedding its warmth impartially on the rags that covered theirs back and on their uncombed heads—a chaotic blending of animal, vegetable, and mineral matter. In the corners of the yard, weeds grew luxuriantly—tall agrimony, all covered with prickles, and other useless plants, whose growth rejoiced the eyes of none but these equally useless people.

In Vaviloff's vodka shop the following scene had been going forward.

Petounnikoff junior entered, leisurely looked around, made a disdainful grimace, and slowly removing his grey hat, asked the landlord, who met him with an amiable bow and a respectful smile—

" Are you Jegor Terentievitch Vaviloff? "

" That's myself! " answered the old soldier, leaning on the counter with both hands, as if ready with one bound to jump over.

" I have some business to transact with you," said Petounnikoff.

" Delighted! Won't you come into the back room ? "

They went into the back part of the house, and sat down before a round table; the visitor on a sofa covered with oilcloth, and the host on a chair opposite to him.

In one corner of the room a lamp burnt before a shrine, around which on the walls hung eikons, the gold backgrounds of which were carefully burnished, and shone as if new. In the room, piled up with boxes and old furniture, there was a mingled smell of paraffin oil, of tobacco, and of sour cabbage. Petounnikoff glanced around, and made another grimace. Vaviloff with a sigh glanced up at the images, and then they scrutinised each other attentively, and each produced on the other a favourable impression. Petounnikoff was pleased with Vaviloff's frankly thievish eyes, and Vaviloff was satisfied with the cold, decided countenance of Petounnikoff, with its broad jaw and strong white teeth.

"You know me, of course, and can guess my errand," began Petounnikoff.

"About the summons, I guess," replied the old soldier respectfully.

"Just so! I'm glad to see that you are straightforward, and attack the matter like an open-hearted man," continued Petounnikoff encouragingly.

"You see I'm a soldier," modestly suggested the other.

"I can see that. Let us tackle this business as quickly and as straightforwardly as possible, and get it over."

"By all means!"

"Your complaint is quite in order, and there is no doubt but that you have right on your side. I think it better to tell you that at once."

"Much obliged to you," said the soldier, blinking his eyes to conceal a smile.

"But I should like to know why you thought it best to begin an acquaintance with us, your future neighbours, so unpleasantly—with a lawsuit?"

Vaviloff shrugged his shoulders, and was silent.

"It would have been better for you to have come to us, and we could have arranged matters between us. Don't you think so?"

"That indeed would have been pleasanter. But, don't you see? there was a little hitch. I didn't act altogether on my own. I was set on by some-one else; afterwards I understood what would have been best, but it was too late then."

"That's just it. I suppose it was some lawyer who put you up to it!"

"Something of that sort."

"Yes, yes. And now you are willing to settle things out of court?"

"That's my great wish!" exclaimed the soldier.

Petounnikoff remained silent for a moment, then glanced at the landlord and said in an abrupt, dry voice—

"And why do you wish it now, may I ask?"

Vaviloff did not expect this question, and was not prepared for an immediate answer. He considered it an idle question, and shrugging his shoulders with a look of superiority, smiled sneeringly at Petounnikoff.

"Why? Well, it's easy to understand: because one must live with others in peace."

"Come!" interrupted Petounnikoff, "it isn't altogether that! I see you don't clearly understand yourself why it is so necessary for you to live in peace with us. I will explain it to you."

The soldier was slightly surprised. This queer-looking young fellow in his check suit was holding forth to him just as Commander Rashkin used to do, who when he got angry would knock out three teeth at a time from the head of one of his troopers.

"It is necessary for you to live in peace with us because it will be profitable to you to have us as neighbours. And it will be profitable because we shall employ at least a hundred and fifty workmen at first, and more as time goes on. If a hundred of these on each weekly pay-day drink a glass of vodka, it means that during the month you will sell four hundred glasses more than you do at present. This is taking it at the lowest calculation; besides that, there's the catering for them. You don't seem a fool, and you've had some experience; don't you see now the advantage that our neighbourhood will be to you?"

"It's true!" said Vaviloff, nodding his head. "I knew it."

"Well then"—

The young merchant raised his voice.

"Oh! nothing. Let's arrange terms."

"I'm delighted you make up your mind so promptly. I have here a declaration prepared in readiness, declaring that you are willing to stop proceedings against my father. Read it and sign it."

Vaviloff glanced with round eyes at his interlocutor, with a presentiment that something exceedingly disagreeable was coming.

"Wait a moment. Sign what? What do you mean?"

"Simply write your name and your family name here," said Petounnikoff, politely pointing out with his finger the place left for the signature.

"That's not what I mean—that is, I mean, what compensation will you give me for the land?"

"The land is of no use to you," said Petounnikoff soothingly.

"Still it's mine!" exclaimed the soldier.

"To be sure. But how much would you claim?"

"Well, let's say the sum named in the summons. The amount is stated there," suggested Vaviloff hesitatingly.

"Six hundred?" Petounnikoff laughed as if highly amused. "That's a good joke!"

"I have a right to it! I can even claim two thousand! I can insist on your pulling down the wall; and that is what I want. That's why the sum claimed is so small. I demand that you should pull it down!"

"Go on with it then! We shall perhaps have to pull it down, but not for two or three years—not till you have been involved in heavy law expenses. After that we shall open a vodka shop of our own, which will be better than yours, and you will go to the wall! You'll be ruined, my friend; we'll take care of that. We might be taking steps to start the vodka shop at once, but we are busy just now, have got our hands full; besides, we are sorry for you. Why should one take the bread out of a man's mouth without a reason?"

Jegor Terentievitch clenched his teeth, feeling that his visitor held his fate in his hands. Vaviloff felt pity for himself, brought face to face as he was with this cold, mercenary, implacable person in his ridiculous check suit.

"And living so near us, and being on friendly terms with us, you, my friend, might have turned a pretty penny. We might have helped you also; for instance, I should advise you at once to open a little shop—tobacco, matches, bread, cucumbers, and so on. You'd find plenty of customers."

Vaviloff listened, and not being a fool, understood that the best for him at present was to trust to the generosity of his enemy. In fact, he ought to have begun by that; and not being able any longer to conceal his anger and his humiliation, he burst out into loud imprecations against Kouvalda.

"Drunkard! Cursed swine—may the devil take him!"

"That's meant for the lawyer who worded your report?" asked Petounnikoff quietly, and added with a sigh: "Indeed he might have served you a bad turn, if we hadn't taken pity on you!"

"Ah!" sighed the distressed soldier, letting his hands fall in despair. "There were two of them—one started the business, and the other did the writing, the cursed scribbler!"

" How, a newspaper scribbler ? "

" Well, he writes for the newspapers. They are both of them tenants of yours. Nice sort of people they are ! Get rid of them ; send them off for God's sake ! They are robbers ; they set everyone in the street against each other ; there is no peace with them ; they have no respect for law or order. One has always to be on one's guard with them against robbery or arson."

" But this newspaper scribbler, who is he ? " asked Petounnikoff in an interested tone.

" He ? He's a drunkard. He was a school-teacher, and got turned away. He has drunk all he had, and now he writes for the newspapers, and invents petitions. He's a real bad 'un ! "

" H'm-m ! And it was he, then, who wrote your petition ? Just so ! Evidently it was he who wrote about the construction of the scaffolding. He seemed to suggest that the scaffolding was not built according to the by-laws."

" That's he ! That's just like him, the dog ! He read it here, and was boasting that he would run Petounnikoff into expense ! "

" H'm-m ! Well, how about coming to terms ? "

" To terms ? " The soldier dropped his head and grew thoughtful. " Ah ! what a · miserable dark existence ours is ! " he exclaimed sadly, scratching the back of his head.

" You must begin to improve it ! " said Petounnikoff, lighting a cigarette.

" Improve it ? That's easy to say, sir ! But we have no liberty ! that's what is the matter. Just look at my life, sir. I'm always in terror, always on my guard, and have no freedom of action. And why is that? Fear! This wretch of a school-master may write to the newspapers about me, he sets the sanitary authorities at me, and I have to pay fines. One has always to be on one's guard against these lodgers of yours, lest they burn, murder, or rob one! How can I stop them? They don't fear the police! If they do get clapped into prison, they are only glad; because it means free rations!"

"Well, we'll get rid of them if we come to terms with you," Petounnikoff promised.

"And what shall the terms be?" asked Vaviloff, anxiously and gloomily.

"State your own terms."

"Well, then, let it be the six hundred mentioned in the summons!"

"Wouldn't a hundred be enough?" said the trader, in a calm voice.

He watched the landlord narrowly, and smiling gently, added, "I won't give a rouble more!"

After saying this he removed his spectacles, and began slowly wiping the glasses with his handker-chief. Vaviloff, sick at heart, looked at him, experiencing every moment towards him a feeling of greater respect. In the quiet face of youug Petounnikoff, in his large grey eyes and prominent cheek-bones, and in his whole coarse, robust figure, there was so much self-reliant force, sure of itself, and well disciplined by the mind. Besides, Vaviloff liked the way that Petounnikoff spoke to him; his voice possessed simple friendly intonations, and there was no striving after effect, just as if he were speaking to an equal; though Vaviloff well understood that he, a soldier, was not the equal of this man.

Watching him almost with admiration, the soldier felt within himself a rush of eager curiosity, which for a moment checked all other feeling, so that he could not help asking Petounnikoff in a respectful voice—

"Where did you study?"

"At the Technological Institution. But why do you ask?" replied the other, smiling.

"Oh, nothing; I beg your pardon."

The soldier dropped his head, and suddenly exclaimed in a voice that was almost inspired, so full was it of admiration and of envy, "Yes! that's what education can do! Knowledge is indeed enlightenment, and that means everything! And we others, we are like owls looking at the sun. Bad luck to us! Well, sir, let us settle up this affair."

And with a decided gesture he stretched out his hand to Petounnikoff, and said in a half choking voice—

"Let's say five hundred!"

"Not more than a hundred roubles, Jegor Terentievitch!"

Petounnikoff shrugged his shoulders, as if regretting not being able to give more, and patted the soldier's hairy hand with his large white one.

They soon clinched the bargain now, for the soldier suddenly started with long strides to meet the terms of Petounnikoff, who remained implacably firm. When Vaviloff had received the hundred roubles, and signed the paper, he dashed the pen on the table, exclaiming, " That's done ! Now I'll have to settle up with that band of tramps. They'll bother the life out of me, the devils ! "

" You can tell them that I paid you all that you demanded in the summons," suggested Petounnikoff, puffing out thin rings of smoke, and watching them rise and vanish.

" They'll never believe that ! They are clever rogues ; as sharp as "——

Vaviloff stopped just in time, confused at the thought of the comparison which almost escaped from his lips, and glanced nervously at the merchant's son. But this latter went on smoking, and seemed wholly engrossed with that occupation. He left soon after, promising Vaviloff, as he bade him good-bye, to destroy ere long this nest of noxious beings. Vaviloff watched him, sighing, and feeling a keen desire to shout something malicious and offensive at the man who walked with firm steps up the steep road, striding over the ruts and heaps of rubbish.

That same evening the captain appeared at the vodka shop ; his brows were knit severely, and his right hand was firmly clenched. Vaviloff glanced at him deprecatingly.

" Well, you worthy descendant of Cain and of Judas ! tell us all about it ! "

" It's all settled ! " said Vaviloff, sighing and dropping his eyes.

" I don't doubt it. How many shekels did you get ? "

" Four hundred roubles down ! "

" A lie ! as sure as I live ! Well, so much the better for me. Without any more talking, Jegorka, hand me over 10 per cent. for my discovery ; twenty-five roubles for the schoolmaster for writing out the summons, and a gallon of vodka for the company, with grub to match. Hand the money over at once, and the vodka with the rest must be ready by eight o'clock ! "

Vaviloff turned green, and stared at Kouvalda with wide-open eyes.

" Don't you wish you may get it ! That's down-right robbery ! I'm not going to give it. Are you in your senses to suggest such a thing, Aristide Fomitch ? You'll have to keep your appetite till the next holiday comes round ; things have changed, and I'm in a position not to be afraid of you now, I am ! "

Kouvalda glanced at the clock.

" I give you, Jegor, ten minutes for your fool's chatter ! Then stop wagging your tongue and give me what I demand ! If you don't—then look out for yourself ! Do you remember reading in the paper about that robbery at Bassoff's ? Well, ' The End ' has been selling things to you—you understand ? You shan't have time to hide anything ; we'll see to that ; and this very night, you understand ? "

" 'Ristide Fomitch ! Why are you so hard on me ? " wailed the old soldier.

"No more cackle! Have you understood? Yes or no?"

Kouvalda, tall and grey-headed, frowning impressively, spoke in a low voice, whose hoarse bass resounded threateningly in the empty vodka shop. At the best of times Vaviloff was afraid of him as a man who had been once an officer, and as an individual who had now nothing to lose. But at this moment he beheld Kouvalda in a new light; unlike his usual manner, the captain spoke little, but his words were those of one who expected obedience, and in his voice there was an implied threat. Vaviloff felt that the captain could, if he chose, destroy him with pleasure. He had to give way to force, but choking with rage, he tried once more to escape his punishment. He sighed deeply and began humbly—

"It would seem the proverb is right which says, 'You reap what you sow.' 'Ristide Fomitch, I have lied to you! I wanted to make myself out cleverer than I really am. All I got was a hundred roubles."

"Well! what then?" asked Kouvalda curtly.

"It wasn't four hundred as I told you, and that means"—

"It means nothing! How am I to know whether you were lying then or now? I mean to have sixty-five roubles out of you. That's only reasonable, so now."

"Ah, my God! 'Ristide Fomitch. I have always paid you your due!"

"Come! no more words, Jegorka, you descendant of Judas!"

" I will give it to you, then, but God will punish you for this ! "

" Silence, you scab ! " roared the captain, rolling his eyes savagely. " I am sufficiently punished by God already. He has placed me in a position in which I am obliged to see you and talk to you. I'll crush you here on the spot like a fly."

And he shook his fist under Vaviloff's nose, and gnashed his teeth.

After he had left, Vaviloff smiled cunningly and blinked his eyes rapidly. Then two large tears rolled down his cheeks. They were hot and grimy, and as they disappeared into his beard, two others rolled down in their place. Then Vaviloff retired into the back room, and knelt in front of the eikons ; he remained there for some time motionless, without wiping the tears from his wrinkled brown cheeks.

Deacon Tarass, who had always a fancy for the open air, proposed to the outcasts they should go out into the fields, and there in one of the hollows, in the midst of nature's beauties, and under the open sky, should drink Vaviloff's vodka. But the captain and the others unanimously scouted the deacon's ideas of nature, and decided to have their carouse in their own yard.

" One, two, three," reckoned Aristide Fomitch, " we are thirteen in all ; the schoolmaster is missing, but some other waifs and strays are sure to turn up, so let's say twenty. Two cucumbers and a half for each, a pound of bread and of meat—that's not a bad allowance ! As to vodka, there will be about a bottle each. There's some sour cabbage, some apples, and three melons. What the devil do we want more? What do you say, mates? Let us therefore prepare to devour Jegor Vaviloff; for all this is his body and his blood!"

They spread some ragged garments on the ground, on which they laid out their food and drink, and they crouched round in a circle, restraining with difficulty the thirst for drink which lurked in the eyes of each one of them.

Evening was coming on, its shadows fell across the foul, untidy yard, and the last rays of the sun lit up the roof of the half-ruined house. The evening was cool and calm.

"Let us fall to, brethren!" commanded the captain. "How many mugs have we? Only six, and there are thirteen of us. Alexai Maximovitch, pour out the drink! Make ready! Present! Fire!"

"Ach—h!" They swallowed down great gulps, and then fell to eating.

"But the schoolmaster isn't here! I haven't seen him for three days. Has anyone else seen him?" said Kouvalda.

"No one."

"That's not like him! Well, never mind, let's have another drink! Let's drink to the health of Aristide Kouvalda, my only friend, who, during all my lifetime has never once forsaken me; though, devil take it, if he had deprived me of his society sometimes I might have been the gainer."

"That's well said," cried "Scraps," and cleared his throat.

The captain, conscious of his superiority, looked round at his cronies, but said nothing, for he was eating.

After drinking two glasses the company brightened up ; for the measures were full ones. " Tarass and a half " humbly expressed a wish for a story, but the deacon was eagerly engaged discussing with " The Top " the superiority of thin women over fat ones, and took no notice of his friend's words, defending his point of view with the eagerness and fervour of a man deeply convinced of the truth of his opinion. The naïve face of " The Meteor," who was lying beside him on his stomach, expressed admiration and delight at the suggestive words of the disputants. Martianoff, hugging his knees with his huge, hairy hands, glanced gloomily and silently at the vodka bottle, while he constantly made attempts to catch his moustache with his tongue and gnaw it with his teeth. " Scraps " was teasing Tiapa.

" I know now where you hide your money, you old ogre ! "

" All the better for you ! " hissed Tiapa in a hoarse voice.

" I'll manage to get hold of it some day ! "

" Do it if you can ! "

Kouvalda felt bored amongst this set of people ; there was not one worthy to hear his eloquence, or capable of understanding it.

" Where the devil can the schoolmaster be ? " he said, expressing his thought aloud.

Martianoff looked at him and said—

" He will return."

" I am certain he will come back on foot, and not in a carriage! Let us drink to your future, you born convict. If you murder a man who has got some money, go shares with me. Then, old chap, I shall start for America, make tracks for those lampas—pampas—what do you call them? I shall go there, and rise at length to be President of the United States. Then I shall declare war against Europe, and won't I give it them hot? As to an army, I shall buy mercenaries in Europe itself. I shall invite the French, the Germans, and the Turks, and the whole lot of them, and I shall use them to beat their own relations. Just as Ilia de Mouronetz conquered the Tartars with the Tartars. With money one can become even an Ilia, and destroy Europe, and hire Judah Petounnikoff as one's servant. He'd work if one gave him a hundred roubles a month, that he would, I'm sure. But he'd be a bad servant; he'd begin by stealing."

" And besides, a thin woman is better than a fat one, because she costs less," eagerly continued the deacon. " My first deaconess used to buy twelve yards for a dress, and the second one only ten. It's the same with food."

" Tarass and a half " smiled deprecatingly, turned his face towards the deacon, fixed his one eye on him, and shyly suggested in an embarrassed tone—

" I also had a wife once."

" That may happen to anybody," observed Kouvalda. " Go on with your lies! "

" She was thin, but she ate a great deal; it was even the cause of her death."

"You poisoned her, you one-eyed beggar!" said "Scraps," with conviction.

"No! on my word I didn't; she ate too much pickled herring."

"And I tell you, you did! you poisoned her," "Scraps" repeated, with further assurance.

It was often his way, after having said some absurdity, to continue to repeat it, without bringing forward any grounds of confirmation; and beginning in a pettish, childish tone, he would gradually work himself up into a rage.

The deacon took up the cudgels for his friend.

"He couldn't have poisoned her, he had no reason to do so."

"And I say he did poison her!" screamed "Scraps."

"Shut up!" shouted the captain in a threatening voice.

His sense of boredom was gradually changing into suppressed anger. With savage eyes he glanced round at the company, and not finding anything in their already half-drunken faces that might serve as an excuse for his fury, he dropped his head on his breast, remained sitting thus for a few moments, and then stretched himself full length on the ground, with his face upwards. "The Meteor" was gnawing cucumbers; he would take one in his hand, without looking at it, thrust half of it into his mouth, and then suddenly bite it in two with his large yellow teeth, so that the salt juice oozed out on either side and wetted his cheeks. He was clearly not hungry, but this proceeding amused him. Martianoff re-

mained motionless as a statue in the position he
had taken, stretched on the ground and absorbed
in gloomily watching the barrel of vodka, which
was by this time more than half empty. Tiapa
had his eyes fixed on the ground, whilst he masticated noisily the meat which would not yield to
his old teeth. "Scraps" lay on his stomach,
coughing from time to time, whilst convulsive
movements shook all his small body. The rest
of the silent dark figures sat or lay about in
various positions, and these ragged objects were
scarcely distinguishable in the twilight from the
heaps of rubbish half overgrown with weeds which
were strewn about the yard. Their bent, crouch-
ing forms, and their tatters gave them the look
of hideous animals, created by some coarse and
freakish power, in mockery of man.

> "There lived in Sousdal town
> A lady of small renown ;
> She suffered from cramps and pains,
> And very disagreeable they were . . ."

sang the deacon in a low voice, embracing Alexai
Maximovitch, who smiled back stupidly in his face.
"Tarass and a half" leered lasciviously.

Night was coming on. Stars glittered in the
sky; on the hill towards the town the lights began
to show. The prolonged wail of the steamers'
whistles was heard from the river; the door of
Vaviloff's vodka shop opened with a creaking
noise, and a sound of cracking glass. Two dark
figures entered the yard and approached the group

6

of men seated round the vodka barrel, one of them asking in a hoarse voice—

"You are drinking?"

Whilst the other figure exclaimed in a low tone, envy and delight in his voice—

"What a set of lucky devils!"

Then over the head of the deacon a hand was stretched out and seized the bottle; and the peculiar gurgling sound was heard of vodka being poured from the bottle into a glass.   Then someone coughed loudly.

"How dull you all are!" exclaimed the deacon. "Come, you one-eyed beggar, let's recall old times and have a song!   Let us sing *By the waters of Babylon*."

"Does he know it?" asked Simtzoff.

"He? Why he was the soloist in the archbishop's choir.   Come now, begin!   *By — the — waters—of—Babylon*."

The voice of the deacon was wild, hoarse, and broken, whilst his friend sang with a whining falsetto. The doss-house, shrouded in darkness, seemed either to have grown larger or to have moved its half-rotten mass nearer towards these people, who with their wild howlings had aroused its dull echoes.   A thick, heavy cloud slowly moved across the sky over the house.   One of the outcasts was already snoring; the rest, not yet quite drunk, were either eating or drinking, or talking in low voices with long pauses. All felt a strange sense of oppression after this unusually abundant feast of vodka and of food.   For some reason or another it took longer than usual to arouse to-day the wild gaiety of the company, which generally came so easily when the dossers were engaged round the bottle.

"Stop your howling for a minute, you dogs!" said the captain to the singers, raising his head from the ground, and listening. "Someone is coming, in a carriage!"

A carriage in those parts at this time of night could not fail to arouse general attention. Who would risk leaving the town, to encounter the ruts and holes of such a street? Who? and for what purpose?

All raised their heads and listened. In the silence of the night could be heard the grating of the wheels against the splashboards.

The carriage drew nearer. A coarse voice was heard asking—

"Well, where is it then?"

Another voice answered—

"It must be the house over there."

"I'm not going any farther!"

"They must be coming here!" exclaimed the captain.

An anxious murmur was heard: "The Police!"

"In a carriage? You fools!" said Martianoff in a low voice.

Kouvalda rose and went towards the entrance gates.

"Scraps," stretching his neck in the direction the captain had taken, was listening attentively.

"Is this the doss-house?" asked someone in a cracked voice.

"Yes, it is the house of Aristide Kouvalda," replied the uninviting bass voice of the captain.

"That's it, that's it! It's here that the reporter Titoff lived, is it not?"

"Ah! You have brought him back?"

"Yes."

"Drunk?"

"Ill."

"That means he's very drunk. Now then, schoolmaster, out with you!"

"Wait a minute. I'll help you; he's very bad. He's been two nights at my house; take him under the arms. We've had the doctor, but he's very bad."

Tiapa rose and went slowly towards the gates. "Scraps" sneered, and drank another glass.

"Light up there!" ordered the captain.

"The Meteor" went into the doss-house and lit a lamp, from which a long stream of light fell across the yard, and the captain, with the assistance of the stranger, led the schoolmaster into the doss-house. His head hung loose on his breast, and his feet dragged along the ground; his arms hung in the air as if they were broken. With Tiapa's help they huddled him on to one of the bunks, where he stretched out his limbs, uttering suppressed groans, whilst shudders ran through his body.

"We worked together on the same newspaper; he's been very unlucky. I told him, 'Stay at my house if you like; you won't disturb me'; but he begged and implored me to take him home, got quite excited about it. I feared that worrying would do him more harm, so I have brought him—home; for this is where he meant, isn't it?"

"Perhaps you think he's got some other home?" asked Kouvalda in a coarse voice, watching his friend closely all the time. "Go, Tiapa, and fetch some cold water."

"Well now," said the little man, fidgeting about shyly, "I suppose I can't be of any further use to him."

"Who? You?"

The captain scanned him contemptuously.

The little man was dressed in a well-worn coat, carefully buttoned to the chin. His trousers were frayed out at the bottom. His hat was discoloured with age, and was as crooked and wrinkled as was his thin, starved face.

"No, you can't be of any further use. There are many like you here," said the captain, turning away from the little man.

"Well, good-bye then!"

The little man went towards the door, and standing there said softly—

"If anything happens let us know at the office; my name is Rijoff. I would write a short obituary notice. After all, you see, he was a journalist."

"H—m—m! an obituary notice, do you say? Twenty lines, forty kopecks. I'll do something better, when he dies; I will cut off one of his legs, and send it to the office, addressed to you. That will be worth more to you than an obituary notice. It will last you at least three or four days; he has nice fat legs. I know all of you down there lived on him when he was alive, so you may as well live on him when he is dead."

The little man uttered a strange sound, and disappeared; the captain seated himself on the bunk, by the side of the schoolmaster, felt his forehead and his chest, and called him by name—

"Philippe!"

The sound echoed along the dirty walls of the doss-house, and died away.

"Come, old chap! this is absurd!" said the captain, smoothing with his hand the disordered hair of the motionless schoolmaster. Then the captain listened to the hot gasping breath, noted the death-like, haggard face, sighed, and wrinkling his brows severely, glanced around. The lamp gave a sickly light; its flame flickered, and on the walls of the doss-house dark shadows danced silently.

The captain sat watching them and stroking his beard.

Tiapa came in with a bucket of water, placed it on the floor beside the schoolmaster's head, and taking hold of his arm held it in his hand, as if to feel its weight.

"The water is of no use!" said the captain in a hopeless voice.

"It's the priest he wants," said the old rag-picker.

"Nothing's of any use," replied the captain.

They remained a few moments silent, watching the schoolmaster.

"Come and have a drink, old boy!"

"And what about him?"

"Can you do anything for him?"

Tiapa turned his back on the schoolmaster, and both returned to the yard, and rejoined the company.

"Well, what's going on?" asked "Scraps," turning his shrewd face round to the captain.

"Nothing out of the common. The man's dying," the captain replied abruptly.

"Has he been knocked about?" asked "Scraps," with curiosity.

The captain did not answer, for at that moment he was drinking vodka.

"It's just as if he knew that we had something extra for his funeral feast," said "Scraps," lighting a cigarette.

One of them laughed, and another sighed heavily, but on the whole the conversation of "Scraps" and the captain did not produce much impression on the company; at least there were no apparent signs of trouble, of interest, or of thought. All had looked upon the schoolmaster as a man rather out of the common, but now most of them were drunk, and the rest remained calm and outwardly detached from what was going forward. Only the deacon evinced signs of violent agitation; his lips moved, he rubbed his forehead, and wildly howled—

"*Peace be to the dead! . . .*"

"Stop it!" hissed "Scraps." "What are you howling about?"

"Smash his jaw!" said the captain.

"You fool!" hissed Tiapa. "When a soul is passing, you should keep quiet, and not break the silence."

It was quiet enough; in the cloud-covered sky, which threatened rain, and on the earth, shrouded in the still silence of an autumn night. At intervals the silence was broken by the snoring of those who had fallen asleep; by the gurgle of vodka being poured from the bottle, or the noisy munching of food. The deacon was muttering something. The clouds hung so low that it almost seemed as if they would catch the roof of the old house, and overturn it on to the outcasts.

"Ah! how one suffers when a dear friend is passing away!" stammered the captain, dropping his head on his chest.

No one answered him.

"He was the best among you all—the cleverest, the most honest. I am sorry for him."

"*May—the—sa-i-nts—receive—him!* . . . Sing, you one-eyed devil!" muttered the deacon, nudging his friend, who lay by his side half asleep.

"Will you be quiet!" exclaimed "Scraps" in an angry whisper, jumping to his feet.

"I'll go and give him a knock over the head," proposed Martianoff.

"What! are you not asleep?" exclaimed Aristide Fomitch in an extraordinarily gentle voice. "Have you heard? Our schoolmaster is"—

Martianoff turned over heavily on his side, stood up, and glanced at the streams of light which issued from the door and windows of the doss-house, shrugged his shoulders, and without a word came and sat down by the side of the captain.

"Let's have another drop," suggested Kouvalda.

They groped for the glasses, and drank.

"I shall go and see," said Tiapa. "He may want something."

"Nothing but a coffin!" hiccoughed the captain.

"Don't talk about it!" implored "Scraps" in a dull voice.

After Tiapa, "The Meteor" got up. The deacon wanted to rise as well; but he fell down again, cursing loudly.

When Tiapa had gone, the captain slapped Martianoff's shoulder, and began to talk in a low voice.

"That's how the matter stands, Martianoff; you ought to feel it more than the rest. You were—but it's better to drop it. Are you sorry for Philippe?"

"No!" answered the former gaoler, after a short silence. "I don't feel anything of that sort. I have lost the habit of it; I am so disgusted with life. I'm quite in earnest when I say I shall kill someone."

"Yes?" replied the captain indifferently. "Well, what then? . . . let's have another drop!"

"We are of no account; we can drink, that's all we can do," muttered Simtzoff, who had just woke in a happy frame of mind. "Who's there, mates? Pour out a glass for the old man!"

The vodka was poured out and handed to him.

After drinking it he dropped down again, falling with his head on someone's body.

A silence, as dark and as miserable as the autumn night, continued for a few moments longer. Then someone spoke in a whisper.

"What is it?" the others asked aloud.

"I say that after all he was a good sort of fellow; he had a clever head on his shoulders, and so quiet and gentle!"

"Yes; and when he got hold of money he never grudged spending it amongst his friends."

Once more silence fell on the company.

"He is going!"

Tiapa's cry rang out over the captain's head.

Aristide Fomitch rose, making an effort to walk firmly, and went towards the doss-house.

"What are you going for?" said Tiapa, stopping him. "Don't you know that you are drunk, and that it's not the right thing?"

The captain paused and reflected.

"And is anything right on this earth? Go to the devil!" And he pushed Tiapa aside.

On the walls of the doss-house the shadows were still flickering and dancing, as if struggling silently with one another.

On a bunk, stretched out at full length, lay the schoolmaster, with the death-rattle in his throat. His eyes were wide open, his bare breast heaved painfully, and froth oozed from the corners of his mouth. His face wore a strained expression, as if he were trying to say something important and difficult; and the failure to say it caused him inexpressible suffering.

The captain placed himself opposite, with his hands behind his back, and watched the dying man for a moment in silence. At last he spoke, knitting his brows as if in pain.

" Philippe, speak to me ! Throw a word of comfort to your friend. You know I love you ; all the others are brute beasts. You are the only one I look upon as a man, although you are a drunkard. What a one you were to drink vodka, Philippe ! That was what caused your ruin. You ought to have kept yourself in hand and listened to me. Was I not always telling you so ? "

The mysterious all-destructive force, called Death, as if insulted by the presence of this drunken man, during its supreme and solemn struggle with life, decided to finish its impassive work, and the school-master, after sighing deeply, groaned, shuddered, stretched himself out, and died.

The captain swayed backwards and forwards, and continued his speech. " What's the matter with you ? Do you want me to bring you some vodka ? It's better not to drink, Philippe ! restrain yourself. Well, drink if you like ! To speak candidly, what is the use of restraining oneself ? What's the use of it, Philippe ? "

And he took the body by the leg and pulled it towards him.

" Ah ! you are already asleep, Philippe ! Well, sleep on. Good-night. To-morrow I'll explain it all to you, and I hope I shall convince you that it's no use denying oneself anything. So now, go to sleep, if you are not dead."

He went out, leaving dead silence behind him ; and approaching his mates exclaimed—

" He's asleep or dead, I don't know which. I'm a—little—drunk."

Tiapa stooped lower still, and crossed himself.
Martianoff threw himself down on the ground without saying a word. " The Meteor " began sobbing
in a soft, silly way, like a woman who has been ill-
treated. " Scraps " wriggled about on the ground,
saying in a low, angry, frightened voice—

" Devil take you all !   A set of plagues !   Dead ?
. . . what of that ?   Why should I be bothered
with it ?   When my time comes I shall have to die
too ! just as he has done ; I'm no worse than the
rest ! "

" That's right ! that's it ! " exclaimed the captain,
dropping himself down heavily on the earth.
" When the time comes, we shall all die, just like the
rest !   Ha ! ha !   It doesn't much matter how we
live ; but die we shall, like the rest.   For that's the
goal of life, trust my word for it !   Man lives that
he may die.   And he dies, and this being so, isn't
it all the same what he dies of, or how he dies, or
how he lived ?   Am I not right, Martianoff ?   Let's
have another drink, and yet another, and another,
as long as there is life in us."

Rain began to fall.   Thick, heavy darkness
enshrouded the figures of the outcasts, as they lay
on the ground in all the ugliness of sleep or of
drunkenness.   The streak of light issuing from the
doss-house grew paler, flickered, and finally disappeared.   Either the wind had blown the lamp
out, or the oil was exhausted.   The drops of rain
falling on the iron roof of the doss-house pattered
down softly and timidly.   The solemn sound of a
bell came at intervals from the town above,

telling that the watchers in the church were on duty.

The metallic sound wafted from the steeple melted into the soft darkness, and slowly died away; but before the gloom had smothered the last trembling note, another stroke was heard, and yet another, whilst through the silence of the night spread and echoed the sad booming sigh of the bell.

The following morning Tiapa was the first to awake.

Turning over on his back, he looked at the sky; for this was the only position in which his distorted neck would allow him to look upwards.

It was a monotonously grey morning. A cold, damp gloom, hiding the sun, and concealing the blue depths of the sky, shed sadness over the earth.

Tiapa crossed himself, and leaning on his elbow looked round to see if there was no vodka left. The bottle was near, but it proved to be—empty. Crawling over his companions, Tiapa began inspecting the mugs. He found one nearly full, and swallowed the contents, wiping his mouth with his sleeve, and then shook the captain by the shoulder.

" Get up! Can't you hear? "

The captain lifted his head, and looked at Tiapa with dim, bloodshot eyes.

" We must give notice to the police! so get up."

" What's the matter? " asked the captain in an angry, drowsy voice.

" Why, he's dead."

" Who's dead? "

" Why, the learned man."

" Philippe ? Ah, yes, so he is ! "

" And you had already forgotten ! " hissed Tiapa reproachfully.

The captain rose to his feet, yawned loudly, and stretched himself till his bones cracked.

" Well, go and give notice."

" No, I shan't go. I'm not fond of those gentry ! " said Tiapa gloomily.

" Well, go and wake the deacon, and I'll go and see what can be done."

" Yes, that's better. Get up, deacon ! "

The captain entered the doss-house, and stood at the foot of the bunk where lay the schoolmaster, stretched out at full length; his left hand lay on his breast, his right was thrown backwards, as if ready to strike. The idea crossed the captain's mind that if the schoolmaster were to get up now, he would be as tall as " Tarass and a half." Then he sat down on the bunk at the feet of his dead friend, and recalling to his mind the fact that they had lived together for three long years, he sighed.

Tiapa entered, holding his head like a goat ready to butt. He placed himself on the opposite side of the schoolmaster, watching for a time his sunk, serene, and calm face ; then hissed out—

" Sure enough he is dead ; it won't be long before I go also."

" It's time you did," said the captain gloomily.

" That's so ! " agreed Tiapa. " And you also— you ought to die ; it would be better than living on as you are doing."

" It might be worse. What do you know about it ? "

" It can't be any worse. When one dies, one has to deal with God ; whilst here, one has to deal with men. And men, you know what they are."

" That's all right, only stop your grumbling ! " said Kouvalda angrily.

And in the half light of early dawn an impressive silence reigned once more throughout the doss-house.

They sat thus for a long time quietly, at the feet of their dead companion, occasionally glancing at him, but plunged both of them in deep thought. At length Tiapa inquired—

" Are you going to bury him ? "

" I ? No, let the police bury him."

" Ah ! now it's you who ought to do it ! You took the share of the money due to him for writing the petition for Vaviloff. If you haven't enough I'll make it up."

" Yes, I have his money, but I am not going to bury him."

" That doesn't seem right. It's like robbing a dead man. I shall tell everyone that you mean to stick to his money ! "

" You are an old fool ! " said Kouvalda disdainfully.

" I'm not such a fool as all that, but it doesn't seem right or friendly."

" Very well ! just leave me alone."

" How much money was there ? "

" A twenty-five rouble note," said Kouvalda carelessly.

" Come now ! you might give me five out of that."

" What a rogue you are, old man ! " scowled the captain, looking blankly into Tiapa's face.

" Why so ?   Come now, shell out ! "

" Go to the devil !   I'll erect a monument to him with the money."

" What will be the use of that to him ? "

" I'll buy a mill-stone and an anchor ; I'll put the stone on the tomb, and I will fasten the anchor to the stone with a chain.   That will make it heavy enough."

" What's that for ?   Why do you talk such nonsense ? "

" That's no business of yours."

" Never mind !   I shall tell of you," threatened Tiapa once more.

Aristide Fomitch looked vaguely at him and was silent.   And once more there reigned in the doss-house that solemn and mysterious hush, which always seems to accompany the presence of death.

" Hark !   They are coming," said Tiapa.

And he rose and went out at the door.

Almost at the same moment there appeared the police officer, the doctor, and the magistrate.   All three in turn went up to the body, and after glancing at it moved away, looking meanwhile at Kouvalda askance and with suspicion.

He sat, taking no notice of them, until the police officer asked, nodding towards the schoolmaster's body—

" What did he die of ? "

" Ask him yourself.   I should say from being un-accustomed "—

"What do you mean?" asked the magistrate.

"I say that, according to my idea, he died from being unaccustomed to the complaint from which he was suffering."

"H'm! Yes. Had he been ill long?"

"It would be better to bring him over here; one can't see anything in there," suggested the doctor in a bored voice. "There may be some marks on him."

"Go and call someone to carry him out!" the police officer ordered Kouvalda.

"Call them in yourself. I don't mind his staying here," retorted the captain coolly.

"Be off with you," shouted the police officer savagely.

"Easy there!" threw back Kouvalda, not stirring from his place, speaking with cool insolence and showing his teeth.

"Damn you!" roared the police officer, his face suffused with blood from suppressed rage. "You shall remember this! I"—

"Good-day to you, honourable gentlemen!" said the oily, insinuating voice of Petounnikoff, as he appeared in the doorway. Scrutinising rapidly the faces of the bystanders, he suddenly stopped, shuddered, drew back a step, and taking off his cap, crossed himself devoutly. Then a vicious smile of triumph spread over his countenance, and looking hard at the captain, he asked in a respectful tone, "What is the matter here? No one has been killed, I hope."

"It looks like it," answered the magistrate.

Petounnikoff sighed deeply, crossed himself again, and in a grieved tone said—

"Merciful heavens! That's what I always feared! Whenever I came here, I used to look in, and then draw back with fear. Then when I was at home, such terrible things came into my mind. God preserve us all from such things! How often I used to wish to refuse shelter any longer to this gentleman here, the head of this band; but I was always afraid. You see, they were such a bad lot, that it seemed better to give in to them, lest something worse should happen." He made a deprecating movement with one hand, and gathering up his beard with the other, sighed once more.

"They are a dangerous set, and this gentleman here is a sort of chief of the gang—quite like a brigand chief."

"Well, we shall take him in hand!" said the police officer in a meaning tone, looking at the captain with a vindictive expression. "I also know him well."

"Yes, my fine fellow, we are old pals," agreed Kouvalda in a tone of familiarity. "How often have I bribed you and the like of you to hold your tongues?"

"Gentlemen!" said the police officer, "did you hear that? I beg you will remember those words. I won't forgive that. That's how it is, then? Well, you shan't forget me! I'll give you something, my friend, to remember me by."

"Don't holloa till you are out of the wood, my dear friend," said Aristide Fomitch coolly.

The doctor, a young man in spectacles, looked at him inquiringly; the magistrate with an attention that boded no good; Petounnikoff with a look of triumph; whilst the police officer shouted and gesticulated threateningly.

At the door of the doss-house appeared the dark figure of Martianoff; he came up quietly and stood behind Petounnikoff, so that his chin appeared just above the merchant's head. The old deacon peeped from behind Martianoff, opening wide his small, swollen red eyes.

"Well, something must be done," suggested the doctor.

Martianoff made a frightful grimace, and suddenly sneezed straight on to the head of Petounnikoff. The latter yelled, doubled up his body, and sprang on one side, nearly knocking the police officer off his feet, and falling into his arms.

"There, you see now!" said the merchant, trembling and pointing at Martianoff. "You see now what sort of people they are, don't you?"

Kouvalda was shaking with laughter, in which the doctor and the magistrate joined; whilst round the door of the doss-house clustered every moment more and more figures. Drowsy, dissipated faces, with red, inflamed eyes, and dishevelled hair, stood unceremoniously surveying the doctor, the magistrate, and the police officer.

"Where are you shoving to?" said a constable who had accompanied the police officer, pulling at their rags, and pushing them away from the door.

But he was one against many; and they, paying

no heed to him, continued to press forward in threatening silence, their breath heavy with sour vodka. Kouvalda glanced first at them and then at the officials, who began to show signs of uneasiness in the midst of this overwhelmingly numerous society of undesirables, and sneeringly remarked to the officials—

"Perhaps, gentlemen, you would like me to introduce you formally to my lodgers and my friends. Say so if you wish it, for sooner or later, in the exercise of your duties, you will have to make their acquaintance."

The doctor laughed with an embarrassed air; the magistrate closed his lips firmly; and the police officer was the only one who showed himself equal to the emergency; he shouted into the yard—

"Sideroff, blow your whistle, and when they come, tell them to bring a cart."

"Well, I'm off," said Petounnikoff, appearing from some remote corner. "You'll be kind enough, sirs, to clear out my little shed to-day. I want to have it pulled down. I beg you to make the necessary arrangements; if not, I shall have to apply to the authorities."

In the yard the policeman's whistle was sounding shrilly; and round the doss-house door stood the compact crowd of its occupants, yawning and scratching themselves.

"So you don't want to make their acquaintance; that's not quite polite," said Aristide Kouvalda, laughing.

Petounnikoff drew his purse from his pocket,

fumbled with it for a few minutes, finally pulling out ten kopecks; he crossed himself and placed them at the feet of the dead man.

"God rest his soul!   Let this go towards burying the sinful ashes."

"How!" roared the captain.   "You! you! giving towards the burial?   Take it back; take it back, I command you, you rogue!   How dare you give your dishonest gains towards the burial of an honest man!   I'll smash every bone in your body!"

"Sir!" exclaimed the alarmed shopkeeper, seizing the police officer imploringly by the elbow.

The doctor and the magistrate hurried outside, while the police officer shouted again loudly, "Sideroff!   Come inside here!"

The outcasts formed a barrier round the door of the doss-house, watching and listening to the scene with an intense interest which lighted up their haggard faces.

Kouvalda, shaking his fist over Petounnikoff's head, roared wildly, rolling his bloodshot eyes—

"Rogue and thief! take the coppers back! you vile creature; take them back, I tell you, or I'll smash them into your eyes!   Take them back!"

Petounnikoff stretched out one trembling hand towards his little offering, whilst shielding himself with the other against Kouvalda's threatening fist, and said—

"Bear witness, you, sir, the police officer, and you, my good people."

"We are not good people, you damned old shop-keeper!" was heard in the creaking tones of "Scraps."

The police officer, distending his face like a bladder, was whistling wildly, whilst defending Petounnikoff, who was writhing and twisting about in front of him, as if wishing to get inside the officer for protection.

"You vile thing! I'll make you kiss the feet of this dead body if you don't mind! Come here with you!"

And seizing Petounnikoff by the collar, Kouvalda flung him out of the door, as he would have done a kitten.

The outcasts moved on one side to make room for the merchant to fall; and he pitched forward, frightened and yelling at their feet.

"They are killing me! Murder! They have killed me!"

Martianoff slowly lifted his foot, and took aim at the head of the shopkeeper; "Scraps," with an expression of extreme delight, spat full into the face of Petounnikoff. The merchant raised himself on to his hands and knees, and half rolled, half dragged himself farther out into the yard, followed by peals of laughter. At this moment two constables arrived in the yard, and the police officer, pointing to Kouvalda, exclaimed in a voice of triumph—

"Arrest him! Tie him up!"

"Yes, tie him up tightly, my dears!" implored Petounnikoff.

"I defy you to touch me! I'm not going to run away! I'll go wherever I have to go," said Kouvalda, defending himself against the constables, who approached him.

The outcasts dropped off one by one. The cart rolled into the yard. One or two ragged strangers, who had been called in, were already dragging the schoolmaster's body out of the doss-house.

"You shall catch it! just wait a bit!" said the police officer threateningly to Kouvalda.

"Well, captain, how goes it now?" jeered Petounnikoff, maliciously pleased and happy at the sight of his foe's hands being tied. "Well, you are caught now; only wait, and you will get something warmer by and by!"

But Kouvalda was silent; he stood between the two constables, terrible and erect, and was watching the schoolmaster's body being hoisted into the cart. The man who was holding the corpse under the arms, being too short for the job, could not get the schoolmaster's head into the cart at the same moment as his legs were thrown in. Thus, for a second it appeared as if the schoolmaster were trying to throw himself head foremost out of the cart, and hide himself in the ground, away from all these cruel and stupid people, who had never given him any rest.

"Take him away!" ordered the police officer, pointing to the captain.

Kouvalda, without a word of protest, walked silent and scowling from the yard, and, passing by the schoolmaster, bent his head towards the body, without looking at it. Martianoff followed him, his face set like a stone.

Petounnikoff's yard emptied rapidly.

"Gee-up!" cried the driver, shaking the reins on

the horse's back. The cart moved off, jolting along the uneven surface of the yard. The schoolmaster's body, covered with some scanty rags, and lying face upwards, shook and tumbled about with the jolting of the cart. He seemed to be quietly and peacefully smiling, as if pleased with the thought that he was leaving the doss-house, never to return—never any more. Petounnikoff, following the cart with his eyes, crossed himself devoutly, and then began carefully dusting his clothes with his cap to get rid of the rubbish that had stuck to them. Gradually, as the dust disappeared from his coat, a serene expression of contentment and of self-reliance spread over his face. Looking up the hill, as he stood in the yard, he could see Captain Aristide Fomitch Kouvalda, with hands tied behind his back, tall and grey, wearing a cap with an old red band like a streak of blood round it, being led away towards the town. Petounnikoff smiled with a smile of triumph, and turned towards the doss-house, but suddenly stopped, shuddering. In the doorway facing him stood a terrible old man, horrible to look at in the rags which covered his long body, with a stick in his hand, and a large sack on his back, stooping under the weight of his burden, and bending his head forward on his chest as if he were about to rush forward at the merchant.

"What do you want?" cried Petounnikoff. "Who are you?"

"A man," hissed a muffled, hoarse voice.

This hoarse, hissing sound pleased Petounnikoff, and reassured him.

"A man!" he exclaimed. "Was there ever a man who looked like you?"

And moving on one side, he made way for the old man, who walked straight towards him, muttering gloomily—

"There are men of all sorts. That's just as God wills. Some are worse than I am, that's all—much worse than I am."

The threatening sky looked down quietly at the dirty yard, and the trim little old man with the sharp grey beard, who walked about measuring and calculating with his cunning eyes. On the roof of the old house sat a crow triumphantly croaking, and swaying backwards and forwards with outstretched neck.

The grey lowering clouds, with which the whole sky was covered, seemed fraught with suspense and inexorable design, as if ready to burst and pour forth torrents of water, to wash away all that soiled this sad, miserable, tortured earth.

WAITING FOR THE FERRY

WAITING FOR THE FERRY

A S my hooded sleigh jolted across the confines of the wood, and we came out on to the open road, a broad, dull-hued horizon lay stretched out before us. Isaiah stood up on the coach-box, and, stretching forward his neck, exclaimed—

"Devil take it all! it seems to have started already!"

"Is that so?"

"Yes; it looks as if it were moving."

"Drive on, then, as fast as you can, you scoundrel!"

The sturdy little pony, with ears like a donkey and coat like a poodle dog, jumped forward at the crack of the whip; then stopped short suddenly, stamping its feet and shaking its head with a sort of injured look.

"Come! I'll teach you to play tricks!" shouted Isaiah, pulling at the reins.

The clerk, Isaiah Miakunikoff, was a frightfully ugly man of about forty years of age. On his left cheek and under his jaw grew a sandy beard; while on his right cheek there was an immense swelling which closed up one eye and hung down to his shoulder in a kind of wrinkly bag. Isaiah was a desperate drunkard, and something of a philosopher and a satirist.   He was taking me to see his brother, who had been a fellow-teacher with me in a village school, but who now lay dying of consumption. After five hours' travelling, we had scarcely done twenty versts, partly because the road was bad, and partly because our fantastic steed was a cross-grained brute.   Isaiah called it every name he could lay his tongue to—" a clumsy brute," " a mortar," " a mill-stone," etc.—each of which epithets seemed to express equally well one or other of the inward or outward characteristics of the animal.   In the same way one comes across at times human beings with similar complex characters, so that whatever name one applies to them seems a fitting one.   Only the one word " man " seems inapplicable to them.

Above us hung a heavy, grey, clouded sky. Around us stretched enormous snow-covered fields, dotted with black spaces, showing where the snow was thawing.   In front of us, and three versts ahead, rose the blue hills of the mountain range through which flowed the Volga.   The distant hills looked low under the leaden, lowering sky, which seemed to crush and weigh them down.   The river itself was hidden from our sight by a hedge of thick tangled bushes.   A south wind was blowing, covering the surfaces of the little pools with quivering ripples ; the air seemed full of a dull, heavy moisture ; the water splashed under the horse's feet. A spirit of sadness seemed diffused over everything visible, as if Nature were wearied with waiting for the bright sun of spring, and as if she were dissatisfied with the long absence of the warm sun-rays, without which she was melancholy and depressed.

"The flood-tide in the river will stop us!" cried Isaiah, jumping up and down on the coach-box. "Jakoff will die before we get there; then our journey will have been a useless torment of the flesh. And even if we do find him alive, what will be the good of it all? No one should force himself into the presence of the dying at the moment of death; the dying person should be left alone, so that his thoughts may not be distracted from the consideration of the needs of his soul, nor his mind turned from the depths of his own heart to the contemplation of trifles. For we, who are alive, are in fact nothing but trifles and of no use to one who is dying. . . . It is true that our customs demand that we should remain near them; but if we only would make use of the brains in our heads instead of the brains in our heels, we should soon see that this custom is good neither for the living nor for the dying, but is only an extra torment for the heart. The living ought not to think of death, nor remember that it is waiting somewhere for them; it is bad for them to do so, for it darkens their joys. Holloa! you stock! Move your legs more briskly! Look alive!"

Isaiah spoke in a monotonous, thick, hoarse voice, and his awkward, thin figure, wrapped in a clumsy, ragged, rusty armiah, rocked heavily backwards and forwards on the coach-box. Now and again he would jump up from his seat, then he would sway from side to side, then nod his head, or toss it back-

wards.   His broad-brimmed black hat—a present
from the priest—was fastened under his chin with
tapes, the floating ends of which were blown into
his face by the wind.   With his hat slouched forward
over his eyes, and his coat-tails puffed out behind
by the wind, he shook his queer-shaped head,
and jumped and swore, and twisted about on his
seat.   As I watched him, I thought how much
needless trouble men take about most insignificant
things !   If the miserable worm of small common-
place evils had not so much power over us, we
might easily crush the great horrible serpent of our
serious misfortunes !

"It's gone !" exclaimed Isaiah.

"Can you see it ? "

"I can see horses standing near the bushes.   And
there are people with them ! "   Isaiah spat on one
side with a gesture of despair.

"That means there is no chance of getting
across ? "

"Oh, we shall manage to get over somehow !
Yes, of course we shall get over, when the ice
has gone down stream, but what are we to do till
then ?   That's the question now !   Besides, I'm
hungry already ; I'm too hungry for words !   I told
you we ought to have had something to eat.   'No,
drive on !'   Well, now you see I have driven on !"

"I'm as hungry as you are !   Didn't you bring
something with you ? "

"And what if I have forgotten to bring something ? " replied Isaiah crossly.

Looking ahead over his shoulders, I caught sight

of a landau, drawn by a troika, and a wicker char-a-
banc with a pair of horses. The horses' heads were
turned towards us, and several people were standing
near them; one, a tall Russian functionary with a
red moustache, and wearing a cap with a scarlet
band, the badge of Russian nobility. The other
man wore a long fur coat.

"That's our district judge, Soutchoff, and the
miller Mamaieff," muttered Isaiah, in a tone that
denoted respect. Then, addressing the pony, he
shouted, "Whoa, my benefactor!"

Then, pushing his hat to the back of his head, he
turned to the fat coachman standing near the troika,
and remarked, "We are too late, it seems; eh?"

The coachman glanced with a sulky look at
Isaiah's egg-shaped head, and turned away without
deigning to reply.

"Yes, you are behindhand," said the miller, with a
smile. He was a short, thick-set man, with a very
red face and cunning, smiling eyes.

The district judge scanned us from under his
full eyebrows, as he leant against the foot-board of
his carriage, smoked a cigarette, and twisted his
moustache. There were two other people in the
group—Mamaieff's coachman, a tall fellow with a
curly head, and a miserable bandy-legged peasant
in a torn sheepskin overcoat swathed tightly round
him. His figure seemed bent into the chronic
position of a low bow, which at the present moment
was evidently meant for us. His small, shrunk face
was covered with a scanty grey beard, his eyes were
almost hidden in his wrinkled countenance, and his

8

thin blue lips were drawn into a smile, expressive at
one and the same time of respect and of derision, of
stupidity and of cunning. He was sitting in an
ape-like attitude, with his legs drawn up under his
body ; and, as he turned his head from side to side,
he followed each one of us closely with his glance,
without showing his own eyes. Through the many
holes of his ragged sheepskin bunches of wool
protruded, and he produced altogether a singular
impression—an impression of having been half
masticated before escaping from the iron jaws of
some monster, who had meant to swallow him up.

The high sandy bank behind which we were
standing sheltered us from the blasts of wind,
though it concealed the river from our view.

" I am going to see how matters stand yonder,"
said Isaiah, as he started climbing up the bank.

The district judge followed him in gloomy
silence; and finally the merchant and myself, with
the unhappy-looking peasant, who scrambled on his
hands and feet, brought up the rear. When we had
all reached the top of the bank we all sat down
again, looking as black and as gloomy as a lot of
crows. About three or four arshines away from us,
and eight or nine below us, lay the river, a broad
blue-grey line, its surface wrinkled and dotted with
heaps of broken ice. These little heaps of ice had
the appearance of an unpleasant scab, moving ever
slowly forward with an indomitable force lying
hidden under its furtive movement. A grating,
scraping sound was heard through the raw, damp
air.

" Kireelka ! " cried the district judge.

The unhappy-looking peasant jumped to his feet, and pulling off his hat, bowed low before the judge; at the same time placing himself in a position which gave him the appearance of offering his head for decapitation.

" Well, is it coming soon ? "

" It won't detain your honour long; it will put in directly. Just see, your honour: this is the way it comes. At this rate it can't help getting in in time. A little higher up there is a small headland; if it touches that, all will be right. It will all depend on that large block of ice. If that gets fixed in the passage by the headland, then all is up, for the ferry will get squeezed in the narrow passage, and all movement will be stopped."

" That's enough! Hold your tongue! "

The peasant closed his lips with a snap, and was silent.

" Devil take it all! " cried the judge indignantly. " I told you, you idiot, to send two boats over to this side, didn't I ? "

" Yes, your honour, you did," replied the peasant, with an air of having deserved blame.

" Well, and why did you not do so ? "

" I hadn't time, because it went off all of a sudden."

" You blockhead! " replied the judge; then turning to Mamaieff, " These stupid asses can't even understand ordinary language! "

" Yes, that's true; but then they're nothing but peasants," sneered Manaieff, with an ingratiating smirk. "They're a silly race—a dull set of wooden blockheads; but let us hope that this renewed energy of the Zemstvo, this increase of schools, this enlightenment, this education"—

"Schools! Oh yes, indeed! Reading - rooms, magic lanterns! A fine story! I know what it all means. But I'm no enemy to education, as you know yourself. And I know by experience that a good whipping educates quicker and better than does anything else. Birch rods cost the peasant nothing, whereas education strips him bare to the skin, and causes him more suffering than can any rod. Up to the present time education has brought nothing but ruin to the peasant. That's my opinion. I don't, however, object to their being taught; I only say wait a little."

"That's it!" exclaimed the merchant, in a tone of voice that denoted thorough agreement. "It would really be better to wait a little; times are hard for the peasants just now. Failing harvests, sickness and disease, their unfortunate weakness for strong drinks, all these things undermine their prosperity, and then, on the top of this, they pile schools and reading-rooms! What's to be done for the peasant under such circumstances? There is nothing to be done for him, believe me."

"Yes; nobody knows that better than you do, Nitrita Pavlovitch," remarked Isaiah. His tone was firm but scrupulously polite, and he sighed devoutly as he spoke.

"I should think so, indeed! Haven't I been seventeen years among them? As for education, my opinion is this: if education is given at the proper time it's all right, then it may benefit people. But if—excuse the expression—I have an empty belly, I don't want to learn anything except, may-be, how to rob and steal."

" No, indeed, there's no good at all in education!" exclaimed Isaiah, assuming an expression of good-natured respect.

Mamaieff glanced at him, and drew in his lips.

" There's a peasant for you, that fellow Kireelka!" cried the judge, turning to us with something almost of solemnity in his face and in his voice. " Just look at him, please. He is anything but an ordinary peasant—he is a rare sort of animal! During the fire on board the steamer *Gregory* this ragamuffin, this gnat, rescued without anyone's assistance six persons. It was late autumn then; for four long hours he laboured in peril of his life, soaked to the skin, for rain was coming down in torrents. When he had rescued six lives, he quietly disappeared; they looked for him everywhere, for they wanted to recompense him, to give him a medal for his bravery; and at last they found him, stealing away to hide himself in the dark woods. He has always managed his affairs well; he has been thrifty; he drove his young daughter-in-law into her grave; his old wife beats him sometimes with logs of wood; he is a drunkard, and at the same time he is pious. He sings in the church choir, and he possesses a fine beehive with good swarms of bees; added to all this, he is a great thief! Once a barge got stopped here, and he was caught stealing; he had carried off three bags of plums.   You see what a curious character he is!"

This speech made us all turn our attention to the clever peasant, who stood in front of us with eyes cast down, and sniffing vigorously.   His gaze was fixed on the elegant shoes of the district judge, and two suggestive little wrinkles played round the corner of his mouth, though his lips were firmly closed, and his face was void of all expression.

"Come, let us examine him.   Tell us, Kireelka, what benefits are to be derived from learning to read?"

Kireelka sighed, moved his lips, but no word escaped from them.

"Come now, you can read!" continued the judge, in a more imperative tone.   "You must know whether learning to read has made it easier for you to live or not!"

"That depends upon circumstances," said Kireelka, dropping his head still lower on his breast.

"But you must tell us something more definite than that.   You can read and write, so you surely can say whether you gain any benefit by it?"

"Benefit, well perhaps.   But no, I think there is more; that is, if we look upon it in the right light, those who teach us may gain something by it."

"What can they gain by it?   And who do you mean by 'they'?"

"Well, I mean the teachers, or maybe the Zemstvo, or somebody."

"You stupid creature!   But I ask you about yourself; for you personally, is it of any use?"

" That is just as you wish, your honour."

" How just as I wish ? "

" Why, to be sure, just as you wish.   You see, you are our masters."

" Be off with you ! "

The ends of the judge's moustache quivered, and his face grew very red.

" Well, you see, he has said little, but I think you are well answered.   No, gentlemen, the time is not yet ripe for teaching the peasant his A B C ; he must be thoroughly disciplined first.   The peasant is nothing but a vicious child ; that is what he is. Nevertheless, it is of him that the foundations are made.   Do you understand ?   He is the ground-work, the base of the pyramid of the State.   If that base should suddenly begin to shake, do you not understand what serious disorder might be produced in the State ? "

" That's quite true," reflected Mamaieff.   " Certainly the foundations ought to be kept strong."

As I also was interested in the cause of the peasants, I, at this point, joined in the conversation, and in a short time all four of us were hotly and eagerly deciding the future of the peasantry.   The true vocation of every individual seems to be to lay down rules for his neighbour's conduct ; and those preachers are in the wrong who declare that we are all egoists ; for in our altruistic aspirations to im-prove the human race, we forget our own short-comings ; and this may account for the fact that much of the evil of the world is concealed from us. We continued thus to argue, whilst the river wound its serpentine course in front of our eyes, swishing against the banks with its cold grey scales of ice.

In the same way our conversation twisted and wound like an angry snake, that flings itself now on one side, and now on the other, in the endeavour to seize its prey, which nevertheless continues to escape. And the cause of all our talk, the peasant himself, who sat there, at no great distance from us, on the sandy bank, in silence, and with a countenance wholly devoid of expression—who was he, and what was he?

Mamaieff again took up the conversation.

" No, he is not such a fool as you say ; he is not really stupid ; it's not so easy to get round him."

The district judge seemed to be losing his temper.

" I don't say he is a fool ; I say he is demoralised ! "

" Pray don't misunderstand me. I say he has no control over himself. No control such as it is necessary to exercise over children—that is where the root of the evil lies."

" And with all due deference, I beg to think that there is nothing wrong with him ! He is one of the Great Maker's children, like all of us ; but, I must apologise perhaps for mentioning it, he is tormented out of his senses. I mean, bad government has deprived him of all hope for the future."

It was Isaiah who spoke in a suave, respectful voice, smiling softly, and sighing all the time. His eyes were half closed, as if he feared to look straight at anyone ; but the swelling on the side of his head seemed to be overflowing with laughter, ready to burst into loud mirth, but not daring to do so. " I for my part urge that there is nothing the matter with the peasant but hunger. Only give him enough good food, and he would soon be everything we could desire."

"You believe he is starved!" exclaimed the judge irritably. "In the devil's name, what makes you think so?"

"To me it seems quite clear."

"For goodness' sake, do tell me! Why, fifty years ago, he did not know what hunger meant. He was then well fed, healthy, humble—h'm! I did not mean that exactly. I meant to say—I—I—myself am hungry just now! And hungry—devil take him!—because of his stupidity. Come now, what do you think of that? I had given orders for the boats to be sent over here to wait for me. Well, when I get here, there sits Kireelka, just as if nothing were the matter. No, really, they are a dreadful set of idiots, I assure you. I mean they have not the least respect or the least obedience for the commands of those who are set in authority over them."

"Well, it would be a good thing if we could get something to eat," said Mamaieff in a melancholy voice.

"Ah, it would indeed!" sighed Isaiah.

Suddenly all four of us, who a few moments before had been snarling irritably at each other over our argument, grew silent, feeling suddenly united by the common pangs of hunger, felt in common. We all turned towards poor Kireelka, who grew confused under our gaze, and began dragging at his hat.

"Whatever have you done with that boat—eh?" Isaiah asked him reproachfully.

"Well, supposing the boat had been here, you couldn't have eaten it," replied Kireelka, with a hang-dog look on his face, which made us all turn our backs on him.

"Six mortal hours have I been sitting here!" ejaculated Mamaieff, taking out his gold watch and looking at it.

"There now, you see!" angrily exclaimed the judge, twisting his moustache. "And this wretch says there will be a block in the ice directly, and I want to know if we shall get off before that—eh?"

It almost appeared as if the judge imagined that Kireelka had some power over the river, and considered that he was entirely to blame for our long delay. However that might be, the judge's question set all poor Kireelka's muscles in motion. He crawled to the very edge of the bank, shaded his eyes with his hand, and with a troubled look on his face tried to peer out into the distance. His lips moved, and he spasmodically kicked out one leg, as if he were trying either to work a spell or to utter some inaudible commands to the river.

The ice was moving slowly down in an ever more compact mass, the grey-blue blocks ground against each other with a grating sound as they broke, cracked, and split into small fragments, sometimes showing the muddy waters below, and then once again hiding them from view. The river had the appearance of some enormous body eaten by some terrible skin disease, as it lay spread out before us, covered with scabs and sores; while some invisible hand seemed to be trying to purify it from the filthy scales which disfigured its surface. Any minute it seemed to us we might behold the river, freed from its bondage, and flowing past us in all its might and beauty, with its waves once more sparkling and gleaming under the sunlight, which, piercing the clouds, would cast bright, joyful glances earthwards.

"They will be here soon now, your honour!" exclaimed Kireelka in a cheerful voice. "The ice is getting thinner there, and they are just at the headland now."

He pointed with his cap, which he held in his hand, into the distance, where, however, I could see nothing but ice.

"Is it far from here to Olchoff?"

"Well, your honour, by the nearest way it would be about five versts."

"Devil take it all! A-hem. I say, have you got anything with you? Potatoes or bread?"

"Bread? Well, yes, your honour, I have got a bit of bread with me, but as for potatoes—no—I haven't any; they didn't yield this year."

"Well, have you got the bread with you?"

"Yes, here it is, inside my shirt."

"Faugh! Why the devil do you put it into your pazoika?"

"Well, there isn't much of it—only a pound or two; and it keeps warmer there."

"You fool! I wish I had sent my man over to Olchoff; he might have got some milk or something

else there; but this idiot kept on saying, 'Very
so-on, very so-on!' The devil! how vexing it all
is!"

The judge continued to twist his moustache
angrily, but the merchant cast longing glances in
the direction of the peasant's pazoika. This latter
stood with bowed head, slowly raising his hand
towards his shirt front. Isaiah meanwhile was
making signs to him. When he caught sight of
them he moved noiselessly towards my friend, keep-
ing his face turned to the judge's back.

The ice was still gradually diminishing, and
already fissures showed themselves between the
blocks, like wrinkles on a pale, bloodless face. The
play of these wrinkles seemed to give various expressions to the river, all of them alike cold and pensive,
though sometimes sad or mocking, or even disfigured by pain. The heavy, damp mass of clouds
overhead seemed to look down on the movements
of the ice with a stolid, passionless expression. The
grating of the ice blocks against the sand sounded
now like a frightened whisper, awakening in those
who listened to it a feeling of despondency.

"Give me a bit of your bread," I heard Isaiah say
in a low whisper.

At the same moment the merchant gave a grunt,
and the judge called out in a loud, angry voice,
"Kireelka, bring the bread here!" The poor
peasant pulled off his cap with one hand, whilst
with the other he drew the bread out of his shirt,
laid it on his cap, and presented it to the judge,
bending and bowing low, like a court lackey of the

time of Louis XV. Taking the bread in his hand, the judge examined it with something like a look of disgust, smiled sourly, and turning to us, said—

"Gentlemen, I see we all aspire to the possession of this piece of bread, and we all have a perfectly equal right to it—the right of hungry people. Well, let us divide equally this frugal meal. Devil take it! it is indeed a ludicrous position we are in! But what else is there to do? In my haste to start before the road got spoiled— Allow me to offer you "—

With this he handed a piece of the bread to Mamaieff. The merchant looked at it askance, cocked his head on one side, measured with his eye the piece of bread, and bolted his share of it. Isaiah took what was left and gave me my share of it. Once more we sat down side by side, this time silently munching our—what shall I call it? For lack of a better word to describe it, I suppose I must call it bread. It was of the consistency of clay, and it smelt of sheepskin, saturated with perspiration, and with the stale odour of rotten cabbage; its flavour no words could express! I ate it, however, as I silently watched the dirty fragments of the river's winter attire float slowly past.

"Now this is what they call bread!" said our judge, looking reproachfully at the sour lump in his hand. "This is the Russian peasant's food! He eats this stuff while the peasants of other countries eat cheese, good wheaten bread, and drink wine. There is sawdust, trash, and refuse of all sorts in this bread; and this is our peasant's food on the eve of the twentieth century! I should like to know why that is so?"

As the question seemed addressed to the merchant, he sighed deeply, and meekly answered, "Yes, it's not very grand food—not attractive!"

"But I ask you why, sir?" demanded the judge.

"Why? I suppose because the land is exhausted, if I may say so."

"Ahem! Nonsense, no such thing! All this talk about exhausted land is useless; it's nothing but a fancy of the statisticians."

On hearing this remark Kireelka sighed deeply, and crushed his hat down on his head.

"You tell me now, my good fellow, how does your land yield?" said the judge.

"Well, that depends. When the land is healthy it yields—well, as much as you can want."

"Come, now, don't try to get out of it! But give a straight answer. Does your land give good crops?"

"If-—that is—then"—

"Don't lie!"

"If good hands work it, why, then, it is all right."

"Ah-ha! Do you hear that? Good hands! There it is! No hands to work the land! And why? What do we see? Drunkenness and slackness, idleness, sloth. There is no authority over the peasants. If they happen to have a bad crop one year, well, then, the Zemstvo comes at once to their aid, saying, 'Here is seed for you; sow your land, my friend. Here is bread; eat it, my good friend.' Now I tell you, this is all wrong! Why did the land yield good harvests up till 1861? Because when the crops were not good the peasant was brought before his master, who asked him, 'How did you sow? How did you plough?' and so on. The master then gave him some seed, and if the crops were then not good the peasant answered for it with a scarred back. His crops after that were sure to be good. Whereas, now he is protected by the Zemstvo, and has lost his capacity for work. It's all because there is no master over him to teach him to use his senses!"

"Yes, that's just it. The proprietors knew well how to make their serfs work!" said Mamaieff, with assurance. "They could make what they liked out of the moujiks!"

"Musicians, painters, dancers, actors!" eagerly interrupted the judge; "they made them whatever they liked!"

"That's quite true. I well remember when I was a boy how our Count's house-servant was taught to mimic everything he heard."

"Yes, that was so."

"Indeed, he learnt to mimic everything, not only human or animal sounds, but even the sound of the sawing of wood, the breaking of glass, or anything else. He would blow out his cheeks and make whatever sound was commanded. The Count would say, 'Feodka, bark like vixen—like Catcher!' And Feodka did it. That was how they were taught then. Nowadays a good sum of money might be earned by such tricks!"

"The boats are coming!" shouted Isaiah.

"At last! Kireelka, my horses! No, stop a moment; I will tell the coachman myself."

"Well, let's hope our waiting has come to an end," said Mamaieff, with a smile of relief.

"Yes, I suppose it has come to an end."

"It's always like that in life; one waits, and waits; and at last what one was waiting for arrives. Ha! ha! ha! All things in this world come to an end."

"That's a comfort, at anyrate," said Isaiah.

Two long objects were to be seen moving along near the opposite bank.

"They are coming nearer," said Kireelka, as he watched them.

The judge watched him from the corner of his eye.

"Do you still drink as much as you used to?" he asked the peasant.

"If I have a chance, I drink a glass."

"And do you still steal firewood in the forest?"

"Why should I do that, your honour?"

"Come, tell the truth!"

"I never did steal wood," replied Kireelka, shaking his head deprecatingly.

"What was it I condemned you for, then?"

"It's true you condemned me."

"What was it for, then?"

"Why, your honour, you see, you are put in authority over us; you have a right to condemn us."

"Ah! I see you are a cunning rascal! And you do not steal plums from the barges either, when they are detained; do you?"

"I only tried that once, your honour."

"And that once you were caught! Wasn't that so? Ha! Ha! Ha!"

"We are not accustomed to that sort of work. That's why I was caught."

"Well, you had better get a little practice at it; hadn't you? Ha! Ha! Ha!"

"He! He! He!" echoed Mamaieff, laughing also.

The peasants on board the boat pushed away with large iron bars the ice which impeded its course; and, as they drew nearer, we could hear them shouting to each other. Kireelka, putting his hands to his mouth, stood up and shouted back to them, "Steer for the old willow!"

Then he hurried down the bank towards the river, almost tumbling head over heels in his haste. We quickly followed him, and were soon on board; Isaiah and I going in one boat, whilst the judge and Mamaieff went in the other.

"All right, my men!" said the judge, taking off his hat and crossing himself.

The two men in his boat crossed themselves devoutly, and once more started pushing away the ice-blocks which pressed against the sides of the boat.

But the blocks continued to strike the sides of the boat with an angry crashing sound; the air struck cold as it blew over the water. Mamaieff's face turned livid, and the judge, with knitted brow and with a look of intense anxiety, watched the current which was driving enormous blue-grey heaps of ice against the boats. The smaller pieces grated

9

against the keel with a sound of sharp teeth gnawing through the wooden planks.

The air was damp and full of noises; our eyes were anxiously fixed on the cold, dirty ice — so powerful and yet so helpless. Through the various noises around us I suddenly distinguished the voice of someone shouting from the shore, and glancing in the direction of the sound I saw Kireelka standing bareheaded on the bank behind us. There was a twinkle in his cunning grey eyes as he shouted in a strange, hoarse voice, "Uncle Anthony, when you go to fetch the mail mind you don't forget to bring some bread for me! The gentry have eaten my loaf of bread whilst they were waiting for the ferry; and it was the last I had!"

THE AFFAIR OF THE CLASPS

THE AFFAIR OF THE CLASPS

THERE were three of us friends — Semka[1] Kargouza, myself, and Mishka,[2] a bearded giant with great blue eyes that perpetually beamed on everything and were always swollen from drink. We lived in a field beyond the town in an old tumbledown building, called for some reason "the glass factory," perhaps because there was not a single whole pane in its windows, and undertook all kinds of work, despising nothing; cleaned yards, dug ditches and sewers, pulled down old buildings and fences, and once even tried to build a hen-house. But in this we were unsuccessful. Semka, who was pedantically honest about the duties he took upon himself, began to doubt our knowledge of the architecture of hen-houses, and one day at noon, when we were all resting, took the nails that had been given out to us, two new planks, and the master's axe to the public-house. For this we lost our work, but as we possessed nothing no one demanded compensation.

[1] An abbreviation or diminutive of *Simon*, used to express intimacy or contempt.—TR.

[2] An abbreviation or diminutive of *Michael*, used to express intimacy or contempt. Bears are nicknamed Mishka in Russia.—TR.

We struggled on, living from hand to mouth,[1] and all three of us felt a very natural and lawful dissatisfaction with our fate. Sometimes this took an acute form, giving us a hostile feeling to all around us, and drawing us into somewhat riotous exploits provided for in the "Statutes on Penalties inflicted by the Justices of the Peace"; but as a rule we were weighed down by a dull melancholy, anxiously preoccupied in the search of a meagre earning, and responded but feebly to all those impressions which we could not turn to material advantage. In our spare time — and there was always more of it than we required — we built castles in the air. Semka, the eldest and most matter-of-fact of us, was a thick-set, Penza-born peasant. He used to be a gardener, but, ruined by drink, as fate willed it, he struck at the town of K—— a year ago, on his way to the Nigny Fair, where he hoped somehow to "get on." His dreams, the embittered sceptic's, took a clear and definite form. He required but little.

"Damn my soul!"[1] he used to say, when we, lying on our empty stomachs on the ground, somewhere in the shade, beyond the town, tried to illumine our future, little by little, but insistently looking into its darkness.

"If I could just cut to Siberia. I'd make my way there, meet a good business-like man, apprentice myself to him directly. 'Take me, mate,' I'd say, 'to share your luck. Pals in prison, pals in hunger.' Then I'd polish off one or two little

---

[1] The Russian exclamation has no English equivalent.—Tr.

jobs with him. That would be something *like*.
Ye-es."

"Why should you go to Siberia particularly?"
I asked him once.

"Why? It's there the real smart ones are, man.
Lots of 'em—easy to find. But *here*—here you
can't for the life of you find a good one. As for
trying alone, you'd only go hang for nothing. Not
used to it. Skill it wants—experience."

Mishka could not express his dreams in words,
but there was not the slightest doubt that he
dreamed continually and persistently. You had
but to look at his good-natured blue eyes, always
gazing into space, at his gentle tipsy smile, constantly parting his thick moustache and beard,
which always contained some extraneous matter,
such as bird's feathers, bits of straw, a shaving or
two, breadcrumbs, pieces of eggshell, etc.; you had
but to glance at his simple open face to see in him
the typical peasant-dreamer. I had my dreams
too, but the direction of my thoughts is even now
interesting to no one but myself.

We had all three met in a night shelter a fortnight
or so before the incident I want to describe, deeming
it interesting. In a day or two we were friends—
that is, went everywhere together, told each other
our aims and wishes, divided everything that fell to
one equally amongst us, and, in fact, made a tacit
defensive and offensive alliance against Life, which
treated us in an extremely hostile manner.

During the day we tried with great energy to find
something to saw or take to pieces, to pull down, to

dig, to carry, and, if such an opportunity occurred, at first set to work with a will.

But, perhaps because each of us in his heart thought himself destined for the fulfilment of higher business than, for instance, the digging of cesspools, or cleaning them, which is still worse, I may add, for the information of those not initiated into that art, after some two hours of the work our ardour somewhat abated. Then Semka would begin to doubt its necessity.

"They dig a ditch . . . And what for?   For *slops*. Why can't they just pour them out on the ground? 'Won't do. They'll smell,' they say. Get along with you! Slops smell! What stuff people do talk, just from having nothing to do. Now throw a salt cucumber[1] out. Why should it smell if it's a little one? It'll lie there a day or two, and there you are—it's gone, rotted away. If you throw a dead man out into the sun, now, he'll smell a bit, to be sure, for it's a big carcass."

Such reasoning and conclusions on Semka's part considerably damped our ardour for work. And this was rather advantageous for us if the job was by the day, but if it was by the piece it invariably happened that we took our wages and spent them on food before the work was finished. Then we used to go to our employer to ask for a " pribavka ";[2] he generally told us to clear out, and threatened, with the help of the police, to make us finish the job already paid for. We argued that we could not

---

[1] A very common food in Russia.—Tr.

[2] Lit., "an addition," *i.e.* additional wage.—Tr.

work hungry, and more or less hotly insisted on the "pribavka," which in the majority of cases we got. Of course it was not exactly honourable, but really it was extremely advantageous, and it is not our fault if life is so clumsily arranged that the honourable and the advantageous nearly always clash. The wages disputes with our employers Semka always took upon himself, and really he conducted them with an artist's skill, detailing the proofs of his rights in the tones of a man worn out with work and exhausted by the burden of it.

Meanwhile Mishka looked on in silence, and blinked his blue eyes, smiling from time to time with his good-natured, kindly smile, as if he were trying to say something but could not summon up courage. He generally spoke very little, and only when half-seas-over was he capable of delivering something like an oration.

"Bratsi!"[1] he would then cry, smiling, and his lips twitched curiously, his throat grew husky, and he would cough for some time after the beginning of the speech, pressing his hand to his throat.

"W-e-ll?" would be Semka's impatient and ungracious encouragement.

"Bratsi! We live like dogs, we do. And worse even. And what for? Nobody knows. But I suppose by the will of God. Everything is done by His will—eh, bratsi? Well, then— So there . . . it shows we deserve to live like dogs, for we are bad men. We're bad men, eh? Well, then— Now I say, serve 'em right, the dogs. Isn't it true what I

[1] Diminutive of "brothers."—TR.

say?   So it shows it's for our sins.   And we must put up with it, eh?   Isn't it true?"

"Fool!" briefly and indifferently answered Semka to the anxious questioning of his comrade.   And the other would penitently shrink up into himself, smile timidly, and fall silent, blinking his eyes, which he could scarcely keep open from drunken sleepiness.

Once we were in luck.

We were waiting for likely employers, elbowing our way through the market, when we came upon a small wizened old lady with a stern, wrinkled face. Her head shook, and on her beak-like nose hopped large spectacles with heavy silver rims; she was constantly putting them straight as her small, coldly glittering eyes gleamed out from behind them.

"You are free?   Are you looking for work?" she asked us, when we all stared at her longingly. "Very well," she said, on receiving a quick and respectful answer in the affirmative from Semka. "I want to have an old bath-house [1] pulled down, and a well cleaned.   How much would you charge for it?"

"We should have to see, barynia, what sort of size your bath-house is," said Semka, politely and reasonably.   "And the well too.   They run different depths.   Sometimes they are very deep."

We were invited to look, and in an hour's time, already armed with axes and a lever, we were lustily pulling down the rafters of the bath-house, having

---

[1] In Russia private dwellings have separate bath-houses, built mostly of wood, and the baths are taken in somewhat the same manner as Turkish.—TR.

agreed to take it to pieces and to clean the well for five roubles.[1] The bath-house stood in the corner of an old neglected garden. Not far from it, among some cherry trees, was a summer-house, and from the top of the bath-house we saw that the old lady sat reading in there, holding a large open book on her lap. Now and then she cast a sharp, attentive glance at us, the book on her lap moved, and its massive clasps, evidently of silver, shone in the sun.

No work is so rapid as the work of destruction. We zealously bustled about among clouds of grey, pungent dust, sneezing, coughing, blowing our noses, and rubbing our eyes every minute. The bath-house, half rotten, and old like its mistress, was soon crashing and falling to pieces.

"Now, mates, hard on it—ea-*sy*!" commanded Semka, and row after row of beams fell creaking to the ground.

"Wonder what book that is she's got. Such a thick one!" said Mishka, reflectively leaning upon his lever and wiping the sweat off his face with his palm. Immediately turned into a mulatto, he spat on his hands, raised the lever to drive it into a crack between two beams, drove it in, and added in the same reflective tone, "Suppose it's the Gospels— seems to me it's too thick."

"What's that to you?" asked Semka.

"To me? Why, nothing. I like to hear a book read—if it's a holy one. We had a soldier in the village, African his name was; he'd begin to reel off the psalms sometimes, just like a drum—fine."

[1] A rouble is about two shillings.—TR.

"Well?" Semka said again, busy making a cigarette.

"Well—nothing. Only it *was* fine! Couldn't understand it, still it's the Word of God—don't hear it in the street like. Can't understand it, still you feel it's a word for the soul."

"Can't understand it, you say. Still you can see you're a blockhead," said Semka, imitating him.

"I know you're always swearing at me," sighed the other.

"How else can you talk to fools? They can't understand anything. Come on—let's have a go at this rotten plank."

The bath-house was falling to pieces, surrounded by splinters and drowned in clouds of dust, which had even made the leaves of the nearest trees a light grey. The July sun mercilessly scorched our backs and shoulders. One could not tell from our faces, streaked with dust and sweat, to which precisely of the four coloured races we belonged.

"The book's got silver on too," again began Mishka.

Semka raised his head and looked attentively in the direction of the summer-house.

"Looks like it," he said shortly.

"Must be the Gospels, then."

"Well, and what if it is?"

"Nothing."

"Got enough and to spare of that stuff, my boy. If you're so fond of Holy Scripture you'd better go to her. Go to her and say, 'Read to me a bit, grannie. For *we* can't get that sort of thing.' Say,

'*We* don't go to church, by reason of our dirtiness. But we've got souls too, all as they should be, in the right place.' Go on—go along."

" Truth, shall I ? "

" Go on."

Mishka threw down his lever, pulled his shirt straight, smeared the dust over his face with his sleeve, and jumped down from the bath-house.

" *She'll* give it you, devil of a fool, you," mumbled Semka, smiling sceptically, but watching with extreme curiosity the figure of his comrade, making its way to the summer-house through the mass of dock-leaves.

Tall and bent, with bare, dirty hands, heavily lurching as he walked and catching the branches of the bushes now and then, he was moving clumsily forward, a confused, gentle smile on his face.

The sun glistened on the glasses of the old lady's spectacles and on their silver rims.

Contrary to Semka's supposition, she did not " give it him." We could not hear for the rustle of the foliage what Mishka was saying to her, but we presently saw him heavily sitting down at her feet, so that his nose almost touched the open book. His face was dignified and calm ; we saw him blow on his beard, to try and get the dust off it, fidget, and at last settle down in an uncomfortable position, with his neck stretched out, expectantly watching the old lady's little shrivelled hands as they methodically turned over the leaves of the book.

" Look at him, the hairy dog ! Got a fine rest for himself. Let's go too ! He'll be taking it easy there, and we've got to do his work for him.   Come on !"

In two or three minutes Semka and I were also sitting on the ground, one on each side of our comrade.   The old lady did not say a word to us when we appeared, only looked at us attentively and sharply, and again began to turn over the leaves of the book, searching for something.   We sat in a luxuriant green ring of fresh, sweet-smelling foliage, and above us was spread the kindly, soft, cloudless sky.   Now and then came a light breeze, and the leaves began to rustle with that mysterious sound which always speaks to the heart, waking in it gentleness and peace, and turning the thoughts to something indefinite, yet dear to man, cleansing his soul from foulness, or, at any rate, making him forget it for a time and breathe freely, and, as it were, anew.

"'Paul, a servant of Jesus Christ,'" began the old lady's voice.   Shaking and cracked from age, it was yet full of a stern and pompous piety.   At its first sound Mishka energetically crossed himself.

Semka began fidgeting on the ground, trying to find a more comfortable position.   The old lady cast a glance at him, but continued to read.

"'For I long to see you, that I may impart unto you some spiritual gift, to the end ye may be established — that is, that I with you may be comforted in you, each of us by the other's faith, both yours and mine.'"

Semka, like the true heathen he was, gave a loud yawn.   His comrade cast a reproachful glance at him from his blue eyes and hung his touzled head, all covered with dust. The old lady also looked at him severely without leaving off reading, and this somewhat abashed him. He wrinkled up his nose, looked sideways, and, evidently wishing to atone for his yawn, gave a long, pious sigh.

Several minutes passed quietly. The improving and monotonous reading acted as a sedative.

"'For the wrath of God is revealed against all ungodliness and'"—

"What do you want?" suddenly cried the old lady to Semka.

"O-oh . . . nothing. If you would kindly go on reading—I am listening!" he explained meekly.

"Why are you touching the clasp with your dirty great hand?" she said, in exasperation.

"I'm curious, for—it's such fine work, you see. And it's in my line. I understand locksmith work. So I just felt it."

"Listen," said the old lady drily. "Tell me, what have I been reading about?"

"Why, certainly. I understand."

"Well, tell me."

"A sermon—so, of course, it's teaching on the faith and likewise on sin. It's very simple, all of it, and—all very true. Just takes hold of the soul—pinches it, like!"

The old lady shook her head sadly and looked round on us all with reproach.

"Lost souls you are—stones. Go back to work!"

"She—seems to be annoyed, mates," observed Mishka, smiling penitently.

Semka scratched his back, yawned, and looking after the old lady, who, without turning round, was walking away down the narrow path, said reflectively—

"The clasps are silver, no mistake," and he gave a broad smile, as if enjoying some pleasant prospect.

Having spent the night in the garden by the ruins of the bath-house, which we had finished pulling down that day, towards noon of the next we cleaned out the well, got soaked in the water, smeared all over with mud, and were sitting in the yard by the porch in the expectation of our wages, talking to each other and anticipating a good dinner and supper in the near future; to look farther ahead we none of us were inclined.

"Why the devil doesn't that old hag come?" said Semka impatiently, but in a low voice.

"Just listen to him!" said Mishka reproachfully, shaking his head. "Now, what on earth is he swearing for? She's a real godly old lady. And he swears at her. What a disposition!"

"We are clever, aren't we? You great scare-crow!"

This pleasant and interesting conversation of friends was interrupted by the appearance of the old lady. She came up to us, and holding out her hand with the money in it said scornfully—

"There, take it and go along. I wanted to give you the wash-house planks to break up for firewood, but you are not worth it."

Unhonoured with the task of breaking up the

wash-house planks, which, however, we were not in need of now, we took the money in silence and went.

"Oh, you old she-devil!" began Semka, as soon as we were outside the gate. "Did you ever? We're not worth it! You dead toad — you! There, go and screech over your book now!"

Plunging his hand into his pocket, he pulled out two bright metal objects and showed them to us in triumph.

Mishka stopped, stretching his neck towards Semka's uplifted hand.

"You've broken the clasps off?" he asked, astonished.

"That's it, mate. Silver! Get a rouble for them at least."

"Well, I never! When did you do it? Hide them quick, out of harm's way!"

"I'll hide 'em all right."

We continued our way up the street in silence.

"That's smart," Mishka said to himself. "Went and broke it off! Ye-es. But the book is a good book. The old lady will be offended with us very likely."

"Why, no, mate, not she! She'll call us back and tip us," joked Semka.

"How much do you want for them?"

"Lowest price—ninety kopeks.[1] Not a copper less. Cost more to me. Broke my nail over it— look."

"Sell them to me," said Mishka timidly.

[1] A penny is equal to four or five kopeks.—Tr.

"To you? Thinking of having 'em for studs? They'll make first-rate ones—just suit your lovely face they would!"

"No; truth—sell them to me!" And Mishka lowered his tone in supplication.

"Why, take 'em, I say. How much will you give?"

"Take. How much is there for my share?"

"Rouble twenty."

"And how much do you want for them?"

"A rouble."

"Make it less to oblige a mate."

"Oh, you fool! What the devil do you want them for?"

"Never mind; you just sell them to me."

At last the bargain was struck, and the clasps were transferred to Mishka for ninety kopeks.

He stopped and began turning them over in his hand, his touzled head bent low, carefully examining them with knit brows.

"Hang 'em on your nose," suggested Semka.

"Why should I?" replied Mishka gravely. "I'll take 'em back to the old lady. 'Here, old lady,' I'll say, 'we just took these little things with us by mistake, so you put 'em on again,' I'll say, 'in their places—on that same book there.' Only you've torn them out with the stuff; how can she fix them on now?"

"Are you actually going to take them back?" and Semka opened his mouth.

"Why, yes. You see a book like that—it ought to be all whole, you know. It won't do to tear off bits of it. The old lady will be offended, too. And she's not far from her grave. So I'll just— You wait for me a minute. I'll run back."

And before we could hold him, he had disappeared round the street corner.

"There's a soft-boned fool for you. You dirty insect, you!" cried Semka in indignation, taking in the meaning of the occurrence and its possible consequences. And swearing for all he was worth, he began persuading me.

"Come on, hurry up! He'll do us. He's sitting there now, as like as not, with his hands tied behind him, and the old hag's sent for the policeman already. That's what philandering round with a ninny like that means. Why, he'll get you into jail for nothing at all. What a scoundrel! What foul-souled thing would treat his mate like this? Good Lord! That's what people have come to! Come on, you devil, what are you standing there for? Waiting? The devil wait for you and take you all, the scoundrels. Pah, you damned asses! Not coming? All right, then "—

Promising me something extraordinarily dreadful, Semka gave me a despairing poke in the ribs, and went off with rapid strides.

I wanted to know what was happening to Mishka and the old lady, and walked quietly towards her house. I did not think that I would incur any danger or unpleasantness.

And I was not mistaken.

Approaching the house, I looked through a chink in the board fence, and saw and heard the following :—

The old lady sat on the steps holding the clasps of her Bible, " torn out with the stuff," in her hand, and looked searchingly and sternly through her spectacles at Mishka's face, who stood with his back to me.

Notwithstanding the stern, hard gleam in her hard eyes, there were soft lines at the corners of her mouth now ; it was clear that the old lady wanted to conceal a kindly smile—the smile of forgiveness.

From behind her back protruded three heads— two women's—one red-faced, and tied up in a many-coloured handkerchief, the other uncovered, with a cataract in the left eye ; over her shoulders appeared a man's face—wedge-shaped, with little grey side-whiskers and a crest of hair on the top. This face incessantly blinked and winked in a curious manner with both eyes, as if saying to Mishka—

" Cut, man ! Run ! "

Mishka mumbled, trying to explain.

" Such a rare book ! says you're all beasts and dogs, you are. So I thought to myself—it's true, Lord. To tell the truth, we are godless scoundrels —miserable wretches. And then, too, I thought, barynia—she's an old lady ; perhaps she's got but this one book for a comfort. Then the clasps—we wouldn't get much for them. But on the book now, they are a real thing. So I turned it over in my mind, and I said to myself, ' I'll go give the old lady some pleasure'—bring her this back. Then too, thanked be the Lord, we earned somewhat yesterday to buy our bread. Well, good-afternoon to you, ma'am ; I'll be going."

"Wait a moment," said the old lady. "Did you understand what I read yesterday ?"

"Did I ? Why, no, how can I understand it ? I hear it, that's so—and even then, *how* do I hear it ? As if our ears were fit for the Word of God ? We can't understand it. You hear it with your heart like, but the ear, it doesn't take it in. Good-bye to you, ma'am."

"So—so !" drawled out the old lady. "No, just wait a minute."

Mishka sighed forlornly, so that you could hear him all over the yard, and moved his weight from one foot to the other like a bear. Evidently this explanation was growing very wearisome to him.

"Would you like me to read you some more ? "

"M'm ! my mates are waiting for me."

"Never mind them. You are a good fellow. You must leave them."

"Very well," assented Mishka in a low voice.

"You will leave them ? Yes ? "

"I'll leave them."

"That's a sensible fellow. You're quite a child. And look at you—a great beard, almost to your waist ! Are you married ? "

"A widower. My wife, she died."

"And why do you drink? You are a drunkard, aren't you?"

"A drunkard, ma'am. I drink."

"Why?"

"Why do I drink? Why, from foolishness. Being a fool, I drink. If a man had brains, would he go and ruin himself of his own accord?" said Mishka in a desolate tone.

"You are quite right. Then cultivate wisdom and get better. Go to church. Hear God's Word. In It is all wisdom."

"That's so, of course," almost groaned Mishka.

"I will read some more to you. Would you like it?"

"Just as you please, ma'am." Mishka was weary to death.

The old lady got her Bible from somewhere behind her, found a place, and the yard was filled with her quavering voice:

"'Judge not, that ye be not judged, for with what judgment ye judge, ye shall be judged; and with what measure ye mete, it shall be meted unto you.'"

Mishka gave his head a shake, and scratched his left shoulder.

"'Dost thou think to escape the judgment of God?'"

"Barynia!" began Mishka in a plaintive tone, "let me go, for God's sake. I had better come some other time to listen. But now I'm real hungry, barynia. My stomach aches, even. We've had nothing to eat since last night."

The barynia shut the door with a bang.

"Go along! Go!" sounded sharply and shortly through the yard.

"Thank you kindly." And he almost ran to the gate.

"Unrepentant souls, hearts of beasts," hissed in the yard behind him.

In half an hour we were sitting in an inn, having tea and kalatch.[1]

"It was as though she was driving a gimlet into me," said Mishka, smiling at me with his good-natured eyes. "I stood there, and thought to myself, oh my goodness! What on earth did I go for?' Went for martyrdom. She might, like a sensible woman, have taken the clasps from me and let me go my way; but no, she begins a-talking. What queer people there are! You want to treat them honest, and they go on, at their own, all the time. I tell her straight. 'There, barynia,' I said, ' here are your clasps. Don't blame me.' And she says, 'No,' she says, 'wait a bit—you tell me why you brought them back to me,' and went ahead as if she was pulling the veins out of my body. I broke out into a sweat, with her talking even—truth I did."

And he still smiled with that infinitely gentle smile of his.

Semka, sulky, ruffled, and moody, said to him gravely when he had ended his Odyssey—

"You'd better die outright, you precious block-

[1] A circular roll made of hard dough.—Tr.

head, you! Or else to-morrow, with these fine tricks of yours, the flies or beetles will eat you up."

"How you do talk! Come, let's have a glass. Drink to the ending of the affair!"

And we heartily drank to the ending of this queer affair.

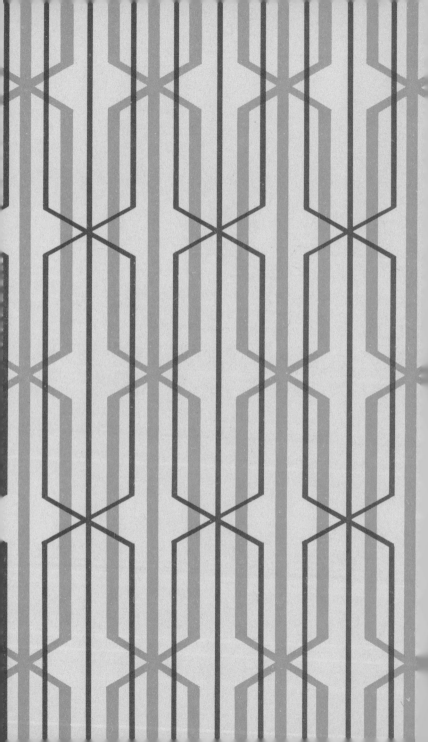